ESSENTIAL
CHEMISTRY

Clive Gifford

Illustrated by Sean Wilkinson and
Robert Walster

Designed by Sharon Bennett and John Russell
Additional designs by Diane Thistlethwaite

Consultants: Michael White, Dr Andrew Rudge
Series editor: Jane Chisholm

With thanks to Steve Mersereau

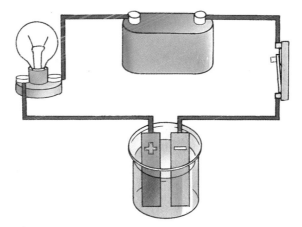

Contents

Using this book

Essential Chemistry is a concise reference book and revision aid. It is intended to act as a companion to your studies, explaining the essential points of chemistry clearly and simply.

The book is divided into sections which cover the main concepts of chemistry. Each section includes the key principles and facts for that topic. Important new words are highlighted in **bold** type. If a word is explained in more detail elsewhere, it is printed in italic type with an asterisk, like this: *bonding**. At the foot of the page there is a reference to the page on which the explanation can be found.

The black and white section at the back of the book offers a variety of reference material, from tables of valencies and densities to details of common experiments. It finishes with a glossary that explains difficult words in the text, and a detailed index.

Examinations

This book contains the essential information you will need when studying chemistry. For examinations, however, it is important to know which syllabus you are studying because different examining bodies require you to learn different material.

Atoms: the building blocks of chemistry

Chemists study the behaviour and characteristics of substances. These are called the **properties** of a substance. All substances are made up of tiny particles called **atoms**. A substance the size of a pinhead contains billions of atoms.

An atom is the smallest unit of a substance that can exist and retain the properties of that substance. There are over 100 different types of atom, known as *elements**. Each element has its own chemical name and a shortened name known as a **chemical symbol**. Most symbols are abbreviations of the chemical name, like H for hydrogen. However, some symbols come from other languages. For example, the chemical symbol for gold, Au, comes from its Latin name, *aurum*.

Molecules

Atoms are rarely found on their own. They tend to group together into particles called **molecules**. A molecule is a particle of a substance which contains two or more atoms *bonded** together. A molecule that consists of two atoms is known as a **diatomic molecule**. Hydrogen, oxygen, and chlorine are all examples of diatomic molecules.

formula. This shows what atoms are contained in the molecule and in what proportions. A chemical formula can also be shown in two other ways. You can use a diagram, like the hydrogen molecule above, or you can use a **structural formula** which shows how the atoms in a molecule are bonded together.

A hydrogen molecule

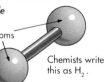

2 hydrogen atoms

Chemists write this as H_2.

It is possible for atoms and molecules to combine with different types of atoms and molecules to create a huge variety of different substances. Chemists give each type of molecule a **chemical**

A water molecule

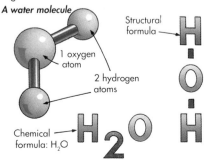

Structural formula

1 oxygen atom

2 hydrogen atoms

Chemical formula: H_2O

Elements, 4; Bonded, 12.

3

Elements, mixtures and compounds

Chemists classify substances as elements, mixtures or compounds.

An **element** is a substance which consists of one type of atom. It cannot be broken down into a simpler substance.

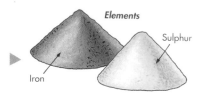

Elements

Sulphur

Iron

Iron filings can be picked out with a magnet.

A mixture

Iron filings mixed with sulphur

A **mixture** is a substance containing two or more different elements mixed together. It can be physically separated with ease.

A **compound** is a substance which contains two or more different elements joined or *bonded** together. This bonding is caused by a *chemical reaction**. A compound cannot be broken down into its individual elements by physical means.

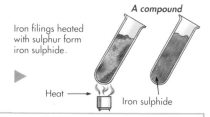

A compound

Iron filings heated with sulphur form iron sulphide.

Heat

Iron sulphide

The states of matter

All substances can be divided into **solids**, **liquids** or **gases**. These are known as the **states of matter**. It is possible for a substance to move from one state to another. This is known as a **change of state**. It normally occurs because of a change in the energy of a substance as a result of heating or cooling.

Many substances can exist in more than one state. In a chemical reaction it is important to know in which state the various chemicals are being used. This is done by placing the symbol (s) for solid, (l) for liquid, and (g) for gas after the name of the substances. A glass of water would be written $H_2O(l)$, whereas ice would be written $H_2O(s)$.

Kinetic theory

All substances are made of particles of matter. **Kinetic theory** explains the changes of state in terms of the positioning and movement of particles.

Particles in a solid are tightly packed and cannot break free from their neighbours. They cannot move; they can only vibrate.

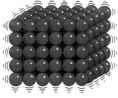

Particles in a solid

Particles in a liquid

When heated, a solid's particles vibrate more and more quickly. Eventually they are able to move around each other, although they can only move within the confines of the liquid.

Further heat gives the particles the energy to escape from the surface of the liquid to form a gas. The particles in a gas are far apart. A gas has no fixed volume; it can expand or be compressed. There is little force holding the particles together, so they are free to move in any direction.

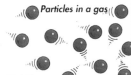

Particles in a gas

4   *Bonded, 12; Chemical reaction, 16.

Evidence of molecules

The molecules in liquids and gases are continually moving in a completely random way. This can be seen when smoke molecules are viewed under a microscope. They move in a random zig-zag fashion because they are being hit by invisible air molecules. This movement is known as **Brownian motion**.

The gradual mixing of two or more different gases or liquids is called **diffusion**. This mixing is caused by molecules of the different substances colliding and intermingling. This is why you can smell perfumes (whose molecules diffuse through the air) from some distance away.

15 minutes later

Gas and air mixed

Boiling and melting

The process by which a solid changes to a liquid is known as **melting**, and the temperature at which the change takes place is called the **melting point**. The process by which a liquid changes into a gas is called **boiling**, and the temperature at which this change occurs is called the **boiling point**. A substance is classified by the state in which it exists at 25°C (known to chemists as **room temperature**). However, two other factors can affect the state of a substance: pressure and purity.

Pressure

The air in the atmosphere exerts pressure on the earth which decreases with altitude. Pressure is measured in **atmospheres**; one atmosphere is the standard pressure at sea level. Boiling points are affected by pressure. The lighter the pressure, the easier it is for particles in a liquid to escape into the air. For this reason, water boils at a lower temperature on a high mountain (where the pressure is lower) than at sea level.

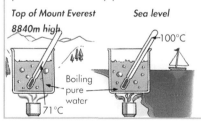

Top of Mount Everest
8840m high

Sea level

100°C

Boiling pure water

71°C

Purity

A substance is **pure** if it contains no trace of any other substance. An impure substance will not have the same melting or boiling point as the pure material. Measuring boiling and melting points is an important way of assessing the purity of a sample.

Freezing and condensing

Unlike melting and boiling, there are some changes of state that require a decrease in energy. **Freezing** is the change of state from liquid to solid. The **freezing point** of a substance is the same as its melting point. **Condensation** is the change of state from gas to liquid caused by cooling. Water vapour in warm air condenses into liquid when cooled.

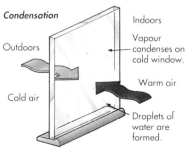

Condensation

Indoors

Outdoors

Vapour condenses on cold window.

Warm air

Cold air

Droplets of water are formed.

Atomic structure

Atoms are made up of particles of matter known as **subatomic** or **fundamental particles**. The three main subatomic particles are called protons, neutrons and electrons. An atom mostly consists of empty space. Almost all of an atom's mass is concentrated in a structure at its centre called the **nucleus**. This consists of protons and neutrons grouped together. Electrons orbit the nucleus.

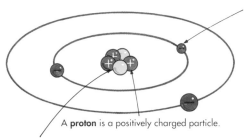

An **electron** is a negatively charged particle. It is kept in orbit round the nucleus because it is attracted to the positively charged protons. This attraction holds the atom together. An electron is more than 1800 times smaller than a neutron or proton.

An atom usually contains an equal number of positively charged protons and negatively charged electrons. This makes it **electrically neutral**.

A **proton** is a positively charged particle.

A **neutron** has no electrical charge.

Atomic number and mass

The number of protons in the nucleus of an atom is called the **atomic number**. This number determines which element the atom belongs to. The total number of protons and neutrons in the nucleus of an atom is called the **atomic mass** or **mass number**. Chemists write the atomic mass and the atomic number in front of the chemical symbol for an element as shown on the right.

15 protons + 16 neutrons = mass number 31

Phosphorus has 15 protons and 16 neutrons.

15 protons = atomic number

Electrons and electron shells

The **chemical properties** of an atom (the way in which it reacts with other atoms) are determined by the electrons. In some cases electrons are passed from one atom to another; in others, electrons are shared between the combining atoms. The electrons in an atom exist in layers called **shells**, or **energy levels**. Electrons are arranged in the shells according to certain rules.

The first shell outside the nucleus holds up to **two** electrons.

The second shell holds up to **eight** electrons.

The third shell holds up to **eight** electrons.

When a shell is full, a new one is started.

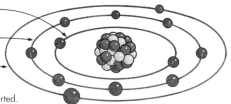

The atomic number of an element tells you how many electrons that element has. An atom has as many shells as it needs to arrange its electrons. The number of electrons in the outer shell determines how *reactive** an atom is.

Atoms like their electron shells to be full. The most stable atoms are those with full outer shells, like helium. The most reactive atoms, like sodium, are those which only need to lose or gain one electron to obtain a full outer shell.

Placing electrons

You can use the rules described on page 6 to determine how electrons are distributed in their shells. For example, the element calcium (Ca) has 20 electrons. Two go into the first shell, while eight go into each of the second and third shells. With the third shell full, the remaining two electrons go into the fourth shell. This information can be written as 2.8.8.2. This is called the **electron structure** or **configuration**.

A calcium atom

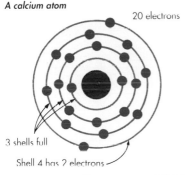

20 electrons

3 shells full

Shell 4 has 2 electrons

Electron structure. 2.8.8.2

Isotopes

Isotopes are atoms of the same element which have different numbers of neutrons. All the isotopes of an element have the same atomic number, but different mass numbers. For example, hydrogen has three isotopes. These are:

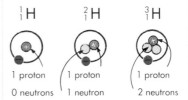

$^1_1$H $^2_1$H $^3_1$H

| 1 proton | 1 proton | 1 proton |
| 0 neutrons | 1 neutron | 2 neutrons |

The isotopes of an element have different *physical properties** but, because they all have the same number of electrons, their chemical properties are identical. A typical sample of an element usually has one common isotope and smaller percentages of other isotopes. A typical sample of hydrogen contains 99.9% $^1_1$H, under 0.1% $^2_1$H and a tiny amount of $^3_1$H. The smaller quantities are known as **isotopic impurities**.

Relative atomic mass

An individual atom of an element cannot be weighed, but its mass can be compared to that of another atom chosen as a standard. One twelfth of the mass of a *carbon-12** atom is used; this comparison is known as **relative atomic mass**, or A_r. The A_r number is very similar to the mass number. However, A_r is a measure of the mass of an 'average' atom of an element. It takes into account the proportions of all the isotopes of an element.

Average atom

$^1/_{12}$th mass of carbon-12

For example, chlorine has two isotopes. One has a relative atomic mass of 35 and in a typical sample of chlorine will make up 75% of the atoms. The other

isotope has a relative atomic mass of 37 and occurs a quarter of the time. The relative atomic mass of chlorine is therefore calculated as follows:

$$A_r (Cl) = \frac{(3 \times 35) + (1 \times 37)}{4} = 35.5$$

With the exception of chlorine, chemists often round the relative atomic mass of an element to the nearest whole number. Relative atomic masses are used to find the relative mass of a molecule. **Relative molecular mass** (written M_r) is the sum of the relative atomic masses of all the atoms in a molecule. For example, the relative molecular mass of a molecule of magnesium chloride ($MgCl_2$) is calculated as:

	A_r of magnesium =	24.3
$2 \times$	A_r of chlorine =	2×35.5
	M_r of $MgCl_2$ =	95.3

The periodic table

The **periodic table** is a structured list of all known elements, arranged in order of their *atomic numbers**. It is based on the work of the Russian scientist Mendeleev, who published his table in 1869. Each element is represented by a block in the table containing its chemical symbol, atomic number and approximate *relative atomic mass**. (A list of symbols with each element's full name can be found on page 55).

Elements in the table can be classified as metals, non-metals, or metalloids. **Metals** have certain properties which distinguish them from **non-metals**. These include generally high melting points, a shiny appearance, and good *malleability**, *ductility** and *conductivity** of electricity and heat. Some elements, such as silicon (Si), have both metallic and non-metallic properties. These elements are known as **metalloids**.

Relative atomic mass ⟶ 7
Li
Atomic number ⟶ 3

Periods

The horizontal rows are called **periods**. All elements in a period have the same number of shells of electrons. As you move down the table, the next period contains elements with one more shell than the last.

As you move from left to right across a period, you find that each element has one more electron in its outer shell than the element before. Lithium (Li), for example, has one electron in its outer shell, while its neighbour beryllium (Be) has two. The change in the number of electrons in the outer shell produces changes in the properties of elements. For example, as you move from left to right across period 2 you find that the melting and boiling points of the solid elements (lithium, beryllium, boron and carbon) increase. The position of an element in the periodic table gives you an idea of its properties.

Groups

The vertical columns are called **groups**. Elements within the same group all have the same number of electrons in their outer shell. They therefore tend to have similar chemical properties. For example, group I elements, with one electron in their outer shells, tend to be very *reactive**.

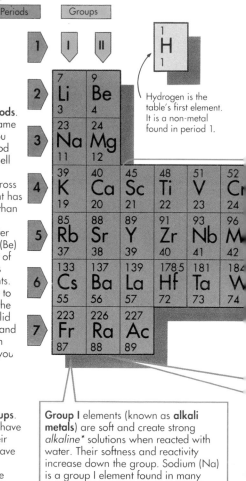

Hydrogen is the table's first element. It is a non-metal found in period 1.

Group I elements (known as **alkali metals**) are soft and create strong *alkaline** solutions when reacted with water. Their softness and reactivity increase down the group. Sodium (Na) is a group I element found in many compounds, such as sodium chloride (salt).

*Atomic number, 6; Relative atomic mass, 7; Malleability, 14; Ductility, 14; Conductivity, 14; Reactive, 14; Alkaline, 25.

Transition metals are found between groups II and III. They are hard, tough and shiny. They are less reactive and have greater densities than group I or II elements. Some transition metals, such as tungsten (W), copper (Cu) and iron (Fe), have a number of different uses. For example, tungsten, is used to make tools and filaments in light bulbs.

Group 0 (once known as group VIII) contains the **noble** or **inert gases**. Their outer electron shells are full, which makes it difficult for them to gain or lose electrons. They are therefore almost totally unreactive. Helium (He) is a very light group 0 element. Being unreactive and *non-flammable**, it is used to inflate balloons.

Key

- Metals
- Metalloids
- Non-metals

Transition metals

					0
III	IV	V	VI	VII	4 He 2
11 B 5	12 C 6	14 N 7	16 O 8	19 F 9	20 Ne 10
27 Al 13	28 Si 14	31 P 15	32 S 16	35.5 Cl 17	40 Ar 18

55 Mn 25	56 Fe 26	59 Co 27	59 Ni 28	64 Cu 29	65 Zn 30	70 Ga 31	73 Ge 32	75 As 33	79 Se 34	80 Br 35	84 Kr 36
99 Tc 43	101 Ru 44	103 Rh 45	106 Pd 46	108 Ag 47	112 Cd 48	115 In 49	119 Sn 50	122 Sb 51	128 Te 52	127 I 53	131 Xe 54
186 Re 75	190 Os 76	192 Ir 77	195 Pt 78	197 Au 79	201 Hg 80	204 Tl 81	207 Pb 82	209 Bi 83	210 Po 84	210 At 85	222 Rn 86

Group II elements have one more electron in their outer shells than group I elements. Although they are reactive, the extra electron makes them less reactive than group I elements. All group II elements, except beryllium, have similar chemical properties. Their reactivity increases as you move down the group. Group II elements are found in compounds which form important rocks in the earth's crust. This gives rise to the group's alternative name, the **alkaline earth metals**.

Group VII elements are known as the **halogens**. They are non-metals and are too reactive to occur on their own in nature. They are usually found combined with other elements in a *salt**. They become less reactive, and their melting points increase further down the group. For example, fluorine (F) is a yellow gas at room temperature, whereas bromine (Br) is a liquid, and iodine (I) is a black solid. Iodine dissolved in *ethanol** is used as an antiseptic.

*Non-flammable (flammable), 58; Salt, 26; Ethanol, 45.

9

The air

Air consists of a mixture of gases (see right), the most common of which is nitrogen. It is possible to turn the gases in air into liquids by cooling them under high pressure. The different gases can then be separated by the process of *fractional distillation**. Many of the *noble gases** found in air are used in different forms of lighting. Argon is used in ordinary light bulbs, xenon in some lighthouse bulbs, and krypton in powerful bulbs used in miners' lamps.

The level of water vapour in the air is known as **humidity**. It varies from day to day and from place to place around the world.

The gases in air

Nitrogen 78%

Oxygen 21%

Other 1% (argon, carbon dioxide, water vapour, noble gases)

Oxygen

Test for oxygen

Glowing wooden splint

Splint relights

Oxygen present

Test tube

Oxygen is essential to life. Without it animals could not breathe and there could be no fire. It is the most abundant element in the earth's crust. Oxygen has a boiling point of -186°C. It is used in many industries, from the burning off of impurities in steel-making, to the provision of emergency breathing units in hospitals.

The gases in air are slightly *soluble**. Nitrogen is less soluble in water than oxygen. Only about 33% of the air in water is nitrogen; the rest is oxygen. If water is warmed it contains less air. The escaping air can be seen leaving the water as bubbles.

Combustion and energy from fuels

Combustion, or burning, a chemical reaction in which a fuel is *ignited** in the presence of oxygen. When a substance burns it uses up oxygen and forms *oxides**. Energy, usually in the form of heat and light, is also given out. A slow form of combustion is also an essential part of the *respiration** process. Combustion of fuels such as coal and natural gas provide us with energy. Below is the equation for the combustion of the gas methane. Energy is also produced in the reaction but is not shown in the equation.

$$CH_4 + 2O_2 \rightarrow CO_2 + 2H_2O$$

Methane + Oxygen → Carbon dioxide + Water

Firefighting

The fire triangle

Fuel

Heat

Oxygen

Three essential ingredients are needed to make something burn: **fuel**, **oxygen** and **heat**. These appear in the fire triangle. Heat is present usually in the form of a spark. Firefighters stop fires burning by removing at least one of these three things. For example, special foams are used by fire services to suffocate a fire by removing its oxygen source. Forest rangers use fire breaks (a corridor cleared of trees) to cut off a fire's supply of fuel. A fire can be made worse if the firefighter does not use the correct method of extinguishing the fire. For example, using water on a *flammable** liquid fire could spread the fire further.

*Fractional distillation, 41; Noble gases, 9; Soluble, 50; Ignite, 58; Oxides, 59; Respiration, 40; Flammable, 58.

Air pollution

Main causes of air pollution		
Pollutant	Effects	Method of control
Soot and smoke	Dirties buildings	Use smokeless fuel. Improve air supply.
Carbon monoxide	Poisonous	Adjust/tune engines. Use catalytic convertors.
Lead compounds	Poisonous	Use unleaded petrol. Reduce lead additives.
Carbon dioxide	Greenhouse effect*	Burn less fossil fuel*. Replant rainforests.
CFCs*	Ozone* depletion Greenhouse effect	Limit use of CFCs. Develop alternative chemicals
Sulphur dioxide	Acid rain*	Burn less coal and oil. Remove sulphur dioxide from waste gases.
Nitrogen oxides	Acid rain	Adjust/tune engines. Fit catalytic converters

Ozone depletion, acid rain and the greenhouse effect are looked at on pages 46-47.

When a substance burns in excess oxygen, **complete combustion** is said to be taking place. **Incomplete combustion** is when combustion occurs in the presence of insufficient oxygen. The burning of hydrocarbon (HC)*-based fuels can result in incomplete combustion. Smoke and soot (both unburned forms of carbon) and carbon monoxide (CO) are formed. Carbon monoxide is a highly poisonous gas that prevents the blood from carrying oxygen.

Many cities like Los Angeles, suffer from serious air pollution. In some cases, a mixture of fog and polluted air forms a **photochemical smog**. This may contain a combination of toxic smoke, soot, ozone and carbon monoxide.

Vehicle exhausts create most of the carbon monoxide released into the air. They also release nitrogen oxides (NO_x), a major cause of acid rain, and lead compounds. Lead compounds are added to gasoline to make its combustion more efficient. However, lead is a very toxic chemical and has been linked with an increased incidence of brain damage in children. Lead is known as a **cumulative poison** because it builds up in the body and cannot be removed.

Pollution control

Most of the air pollution discussed above is caused by vehicles burning fuels.

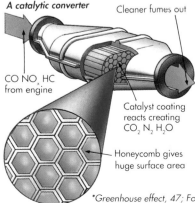

A catalytic converter

Cleaner fumes out

CO NO_x HC from engine

Catalyst coating reacts creating CO_2 N_2 H_2O

Honeycomb gives huge surface area

One solution is to cut down the amount of travelling in motor vehicles. This can be done in practical ways such as car-sharing, living closer to work, using public transport more, and increasing the efficiency of engines.

Most new cars are now capable of using lead-free petrol and many can be fitted with a device called a **catalytic converter**. This contains a catalyst* which heavily reduces carbon monoxide emissions and can cut down soot, smoke and nitrogen oxides. A catalytic converter can only work with lead-free petrol, as lead prevents metals in the catalyst (palladium, platinum and rhodium) from working properly.

*Greenhouse effect, 47; Fossil fuels, 40; CFCs, 47; Ozone, 47; Acid rain, 46; Hydrocarbons, 40; Catalyst, 35.

Bonding

Atoms with a full outer shell are more stable than atoms with an incomplete one. In order to become stable, atoms with an incomplete outer shell attempt to join chemically with other atoms. This is called **bonding**. The three main types of bonding are ionic (where a metal and non-metal combine), metallic (where atoms of one metal combine) and covalent (where two non-metals bond).

In order to bond with other atoms in a chemical reaction, atoms lose, gain or share electrons. The number of electrons involved is called an atom's **combining power**, or **valency**. For example, sodium needs to lose one electron to obtain a full outer shell, while chlorine needs to gain one. Both have a valency of one. Valencies tend to be related to an element's position in the periodic table. For example, all group I elements have a valency of one. Some elements have more than one valency. The relevant valency is written in Roman numerals after the element. You can find the valencies of elements on page 55.

Ionic bonding

When an atom loses or gains electrons it becomes electrically charged and is known as an **ion**. A positive ion is called a **cation**; a negative ion is called an **anion**. The joining together of ions is called **ionic bonding**. Ions with opposite charges are pulled towards each other, this is known as **electrostatic attraction**. This is shown opposite.

For example, a sodium atom can lose an electron to form a positive ion (Na^+). A chlorine atom can accept an electron to become a negative ion (Cl^-). Each ion now has a complete outer shell of electrons. The sodium

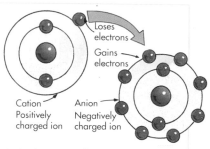

Loses electrons

Gains electrons

Cation
Positively charged ion

Anion
Negatively charged ion

ion's electron configuration is 2.8; the chlorine ion's configuration is 2.8.8. The ions are drawn together and bond, forming a molecule of sodium chloride (NaCl). This is shown below.

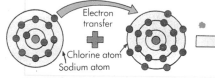

Electron transfer

Chlorine atom
Sodium atom

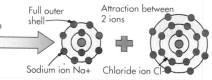

Full outer shell

Attraction between 2 ions

Sodium ion Na+   Chloride ion Cl-

Ionic lattices

Ionic compounds are formed from positive metal ions and negative non-metal ions. When a number of these ions all react together they form an **ionic lattice**. The forces which hold an ionic lattice together are very strong.

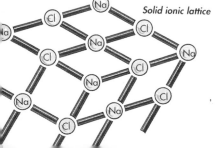

Solid ionic lattice

Ionic equations

An **ionic equation** shows the transfer of electrons, written as e^-. An ion is written with its charge shown after its chemical symbol. For example, magnesium has a valency of 2. When it loses two electrons to form an ion, it is written as Mg^{2+}. Here is an ionic equation showing the formation of magnesium oxide.

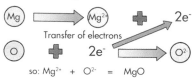

Mg → Mg^{2+} + $2e^-$

Transfer of electrons

O + $2e^-$ → O^{2-}

so: Mg^{2+} + O^{2-} = MgO

Covalent bonding

The atoms of some elements, such as those in the middle of the periodic table, do not lose or gain electrons easily. Instead atoms of such elements form bonds by sharing electrons. This is called **covalent bonding**. For example, a hydrogen molecule consists of two hydrogen atoms each sharing its one electron with the other, giving both a stable outer shell. The atoms in carbon dioxide are also covalently bonded. Each of the oxygen atoms shares two pairs of electrons with the carbon atom. This is called a **double bond**.

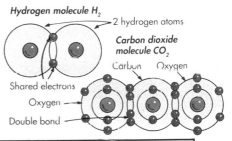

Hydrogen molecule H_2

2 hydrogen atoms

Shared electrons

Carbon dioxide molecule CO_2

Carbon   Oxygen

Oxygen

Double bond

Properties of ionic and covalent compounds

Ionic	Covalent
Formed by swapping electrons	Formed by sharing electrons
High melting and boiling points	Often lower melting and boiling points
Form lattices	No lattices, except diamond and graphite
Dissolve in water	Do not dissolve in water
Do not dissolve in organic solvents	Dissolve in organic solvents
Conduct electricity when melted or dissolved in water	Do not conduct electricity (graphite is the only exception)
Strong forces holding whole compound together	Atoms in molecule hold by strong forces but forces between molecules weak

Metallic bonding

Atoms of a metal can form a lattice similar to that found in ionic compounds. The lattice of a metal is formed when the atoms share their outer electrons to create what is called a **sea of electrons**, or **delocalized electrons**. These electrons can move through the lattice; this enables metals to conduct heat and electricity. The forces holding the lattice together are very strong, which is why metals tend to have high melting and boiling points.

Metallic lattice

Metal cations

Delocalized electrons are free to move within lattice.

Giant molecular lattices

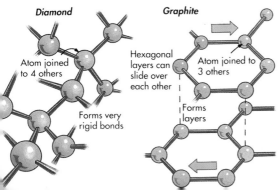

Diamond

Atom joined to 4 others

Forms very rigid bonds

Graphite

Hexagonal layers can slide over each other

Atom joined to 3 others

Forms layers

Some non-metals form a sort of lattice in which atoms of the same type are held together with covalent bonds. This is called a **giant molecular lattice**. A good example, is carbon which forms two different lattices: diamond (which is hard and tough) and graphite (which is smooth and flaky).

Metals

More than three-quarters of all elements are metals. Some metals, such as gold, can be found in a pure state in nature. These metals are relatively unreactive and do not combine easily with other substances. Most metals, however, are found combined with other elements in compounds known as **ores**. For instance, aluminium, a very common metal, is only found in ores. Ores are mined and the metal is then extracted and purified.

The most common aluminium ore is bauxite (Al_2O_3).

The properties of metals

Mercury, used in thermometers, is the only metal which is a liquid at room temperature; the rest are all solids. Metals conduct heat and electricity because of the way their atoms are *bonded** together. The harder metals produce a ringing sound when they are hit. Here are some other properties of metals.

Most metals are shiny and silvery grey. They have what chemists call a **metallic lustre**.

Copper is unusual in having an orange-red colour.

Metals can be drawn into wires. This property is called **ductility**.

Metals can be beaten flat into sheets. This property is called **malleability**.

Transition metals

Many of the most commonly used metals, such as iron and silver, belong to a group called **transition metals**, found in the middle of the periodic table. Transition metals have more than one *valency**. For instance, copper can have a valency of +1 or +2. The compounds that they form are often brightly coloured, like potassium dichromate ($K_2Cr_2O_7$), the orange compound of chromium (Cr). Transition metals make good *catalysts**.

The reactivity series

Many metals react with water, with dilute acids and with the oxygen in the air. Metals can be listed in order of how reactive they are. This is known as the **reactivity series**. (A complete reactivity series can be found on page 49). The position of a metal in the series determines the ease with which it can be extracted from its ore. The more reactive the metal, the more difficult it is to extract.

Here is a general reactivity series for some common metals. Hydrogen, although a non-metal, is usually included because it can behave like a metal.

Most reactive
Potassium
Sodium
Calcium
Magnesium
Aluminium
Zinc
Iron
Hydrogen
Copper
Silver
Gold
Platinum
Least reactive

The most reactive metals, like sodium and potassium, have to be stored in oil as they react rapidly with air and water.

Sodium

Covered by oil

Copper is the least reactive metal that can be produced at a reasonable cost. It is much more common than gold and so is cheaper. It is used for water tanks, pipes and electrical wiring.

Copper

Silver, gold and platinum are the least reactive metals. However they are rare, which makes them expensive and highly prized.

*Bonded, 12; Valency, 12; Catalysts, 35.

Alloys

Metals can be combined by being heated until they are in a liquid state, then mixed together. This forms a substance called an **alloy**. One important alloy is steel*, which is a mixture of a metal (iron) and a non-metal (carbon). Alloys can be created with properties that make them more useful for specific purposes than pure metals. For example, solder, made from tin and lead, has a very low melting point and is used to join electrical components.

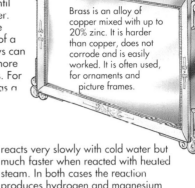

Brass is an alloy of copper mixed with up to 20% zinc. It is harder than copper, does not corrode and is easily worked. It is often used, for ornaments and picture frames.

Reactions with water

When reacted with water, group I metals produce hydrogen and a metal hydroxide*. The metal hydroxide is water-soluble and produces an alkaline* solution. As you move down group I of the periodic table, the metals become increasingly reactive towards water. For example, sodium, in the middle of group I, reacts vigorously. This is shown in the following equation:

$$Na + H_2O \longrightarrow NaOH + \frac{1}{2} H_2$$
Sodium   Water   Sodium   Hydrogen
                  hydroxide

Caesium, at the bottom of group I, reacts explosively in cold water.

Group II metals react less vigorously with water. Magnesium, for example,

reacts very slowly with cold water but much faster when reacted with heated steam. In both cases the reaction produces hydrogen and magnesium oxide:

$$Mg + H_2O \longrightarrow MgO + H_2$$

Zinc reacts in a very similar way to magnesium, producing zinc oxide which is found in many skin creams.

Some transition metals, such as gold and silver, barely react with water, even over a long period of time.

Old gold coins recovered from the sea still look new.

Reactions with air

Calcium reacts with air giving off a bright red light. It is used in fireworks.

Gold and silver do not react when exposed to the gases in the air, nor do they burn. Copper reacts very slowly. It may take years before a green coloured oxide* covers its surface. However when copper is burned fiercely, black copper oxide (CuO) is produced. A number of other metals, including magnesium and sodium, burn in air to form metal oxides.

Reactions with dilute acids

Many metals react with dilute acids (except nitric acid) to produce a metallic salt* and hydrogen. For example:

$$Zn + 2HCl \longrightarrow ZnCl_2 + H_2$$

Zinc + Hydrochloric → Zinc + Hydrogen
        acid   chloride

When dilute sulphuric acid is reacted with a metal, it will produce hydrogen and a metallic sulphate. As you move down the reactivity series, the reactions become slower, until you reach copper at the bottom which does not react at all.

* Steel, 20; Hydroxide, 58; Alkaline, 25; Oxide, 59; Salt, 26.

Chemical reactions

In a physical change the substance may change its shape or its *state*, but it is still the same substance. Water boiling to steam is an example of a physical change. However in a **chemical change**, or **chemical reaction**, a substance is converted into one or more different substances. When sodium and chlorine react to produce sodium chloride, a chemical reaction has taken place.

Equations

Any chemical reaction can be written in an abbreviated form, called an **equation**. An equation shows the **reactants** or **reagents** (the substances that take part in the reaction) and the **products** (the substances produced by the reaction), separated by an arrow. If a *catalyst* is involved, it is shown above the arrow. An equation in which each substance is given its full name is known as a **word equation** and is shown below.

A word equation

Carbon + Lead (II) oxide → Carbon dioxide + Lead

Reactants on the left   Products on the right

Law of conservation of mass

A basic law of chemistry is that you cannot create or destroy matter in a chemical reaction. This is called the **law of conservation of mass**. This means that although substances change into other substances in a chemical reaction, the actual number of atoms remains the same. The number of atoms of products after a reaction will always equal the number of atoms of reactants before the reaction took place. For example:

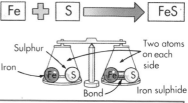

Fe + S → FeS

Sulphur
Iron
Two atoms on each side
Bond
Iron sulphide

Balancing equations

In an exam you may be given an equation like this one for water.

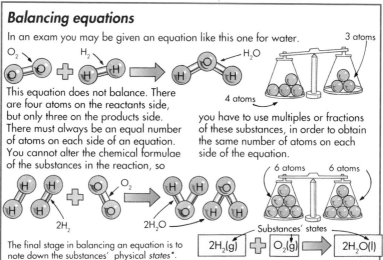

O₂   H₂   H₂O
3 atoms

This equation does not balance. There are four atoms on the reactants side, but only three on the products side. There must always be an equal number of atoms on each side of an equation. You cannot alter the chemical formulae of the substances in the reaction, so

4 atoms

you have to use multiples or fractions of these substances, in order to obtain the same number of atoms on each side of the equation.

6 atoms   6 atoms

$2H_2$ $2H_2O$

Substances' states

$2H_2(g)$ + $O_2(g)$ → $2H_2O(l)$

The final stage in balancing an equation is to note down the substances' physical *states*.

State, 4; Catalyst, 35.

Types of chemical reaction

There are three main types of chemical reaction: thermal decomposition, displacement, and redox reactions (see page 18). These three types account for nearly all the chemical reactions that can take place.

Thermal decomposition

Thermal decomposition is a reaction in which a substance breaks down when it is heated, and the products do not recombine on cooling. Compounds formed from less reactive elements have weaker bonds between their atoms. They are more readily decomposed by this method than those formed by more reactive elements.

Two examples of thermal decomposition are the reactions of sodium nitrate and calcium nitrate when heated (see opposite).

$$NaNO_3 \implies NaNO_2 + \tfrac{1}{2}O_2$$

Sodium nitrate — Sodium nitrite — Oxygen

You can test for oxygen with a glowing splint. If it relights it shows that oxygen is present.

$$2Ca(NO_3)_2 \implies 2CaO + O_2 + 4NO_2$$

Calcium nitrate — Calcium oxide — Oxygen — Nitrogen dioxide

Nitrogen dioxide is a a brown, acidic gas which can be easily identified.

Displacement reactions

A reaction in which one element replaces another in a compound is called a **displacement reaction** An element will only displace another element lower than itself in the reactivity series. The reaction opposite occurs if iron is put in copper sulphate solution. Iron is higher than copper in the series so it pushes the copper out of the solution.

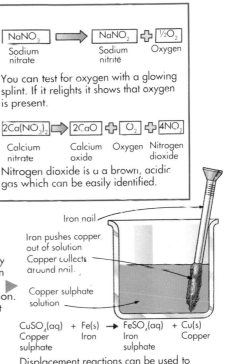

Iron nail
Iron pushes copper out of solution
Copper collects around nail.
Copper sulphate solution

$$CuSO_4(aq) + Fe(s) \rightarrow FeSO_4(aq) + Cu(s)$$

Copper sulphate — Iron — Iron sulphate — Copper

Displacement reactions can be used to identify an unknown metal by finding its place in the reactivity series. The metal is placed in a series of known metal ion* solutions. Those the metal displaces are below it in the reactivity series; those it does not displace are above it.

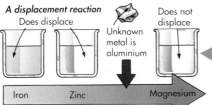

A displacement reaction

Does displace — Does not displace

Unknown metal is aluminium

Iron — Zinc — Magnesium

Reversible reactions

A reaction that does not convert all of its reagent into product is known as a reversible reaction. The symbol $\rightleftharpoons$ is used to show a reversible reaction.

For example, the thermal decomposition of ammonium chloride involves a **reversible reaction**. When heated, the substance produces two gases, hydrogen chloride (HCl) and ammonia (NH_3). These two gases react together to produce ammonium chloride. This reaction can go forwards or backwards. Some of each substance will always remain.

$$NH_4Cl(s) \rightleftharpoons NH_3(g) + HCl(g)$$

Reversible reaction symbol

*Ion, 12.

Reduction and oxidation

Reduction and oxidation are reactions which involve electrons moving from one atom to another. One or more of the actions in the table opposite occur during such a reaction.

Oxidation and reduction take place simultaneously; this is known as a **redox reaction**. If one substance loses electrons, or atoms of oxygen or hydrogen, then another substance must gain them. There is an example of this in the equation opposite.

Oxidation	Reduction
Electrons lost Hydrogen lost Oxygen gained	Electrons gained Hydrogen gained Oxygen lost

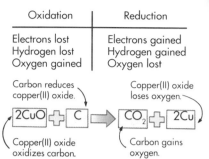

Carbon reduces copper(II) oxide.

Copper(II) oxide loses oxygen.

$$2CuO + C \rightarrow CO_2 + 2Cu$$

Copper(II) oxide oxidizes carbon.

Carbon gains oxygen.

Electron swapping

Redox reactions always involve the swapping of electrons. The electrons are either on their own, or within hydrogen or oxygen atoms which are exchanged between substances in a reaction. The reduction and oxidation reactions can each be shown as half of an *ionic equation**. These are called **half equations**. In the example below, magnesium and chlorine undergo a redox reaction to form magnesium chloride.

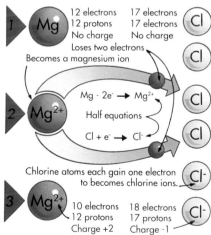

1 Mg | 12 electrons 17 electrons | Cl
       12 protons   17 electrons
       No charge   No charge

Loses two electrons
Becomes a magnesium ion

2 Mg^{2+} | Mg - 2e$^-$ → Mg^{2+}
           Half equations
           Cl + e$^-$ → Cl$^-$

Chlorine atoms each gain one electron to becomes chlorine ions.

3 Mg^{2+} | 10 electrons 18 electrons | Cl$^-$
             12 protons   17 protons
             Charge +2   Charge -1

Oxidation numbers

All elements in compounds have an **oxidation number**. This is the number of electrons that have been added or taken away from the neutral atom to create the positively or negatively charged ion. The oxidation number increases (it becomes more positive or less negative) during oxidation and decreases (it becomes less positive or more negative) during reduction. The oxidation number is the same as the *valency** of an element. (See page 55 for a list of oxidation numbers).

The oxidation number of an element in its neutral state, such as fluorine gas or solid copper, is zero. The sum of the oxidation states of all the atoms in a compound will also equal zero.

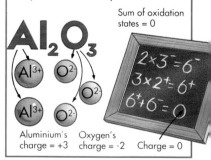

Sum of oxidation states = 0

Al_2O_3

Aluminium's charge = +3

Oxygen's charge = -2

Charge = 0

$2 \times 3 = 6^-$
$3 \times 2 = 6^+$
$6^+ + 6^- = 0$

Oxidizing and reducing agents

A substance that oxidizes another substance is called an **oxidizing agent**. Common oxidizing agents are hydrogen peroxide, oxygen and chlorine. A **reducing agent** is a substance which reduces another. Reducing agents are used in industry to reduce metal oxides to pure metal. For example, carbon, in coke form, is used to reduce zinc and iron oxides to their pure metals.

*Ionic equation, 12; Valency, 12.

Resources

The substances found in nature which can be processed to provide the things we need and use in life are known as **resources**. There are many different resource types, but they come from the four main sources shown here.

| From water **(the hydrosphere)** | From air **(the atmosphere)** | From rocks **(the lithosphere)** | From living things **(the biosphere)** |

Renewable and non-renewable resources

Renewable resources, such as plants and wave power, are those which can be replaced as they are used. However these will run out if they are not replaced fast enough. For example, forests will be exhausted if new trees are not planted quickly enough to replace felled ones. **Non-renewable resources** such as gold or tin are not replaceable and will run out.

The amount of a resource worth extracting is called its reserve. The reserve depends on the cost of extraction and the price at which it can be sold. For example, there is still tin in mines in South West England but the price of tin is not high enough to make its extraction worthwhile.

Conserving resources

It is important to conserve all our resources. This can be done in several ways, as shown below.

One way is to avoid waste and use materials more carefully. New techniques and designs can help to reduce the amount of a resource used. For example, cars are now being designed to be more efficient.

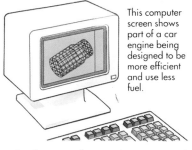

This computer screen shows part of a car engine being designed to be more efficient and use less fuel.

Another way of conserving resources is to adapt common resources to take the place of less plentiful ones. For example, plastic pipes and guttering are replacing pipes made from less common resources such as copper and lead.

Recycling

Instead of being disposed of after first use, some materials are now being reused. This is known as **recycling**. Paper, glass, iron and aluminium are all being increasingly recycled.

Recycled paper products

Old paper is collected and processed back into all kinds of paper products.

Recycling means that less new material is being used, so there is less waste to dispose of. It also means that energy normally used in extracting the material is saved. It is estimated that for every tonne (1.016 tons) of recycled glass used, the equivalent of 136.5 litres (36 US gallons) of oil is saved.

Bottle banks are now popular in many countries. The collected glass is sorted, melted and then re-used.

Iron and steel

Iron is the most important metal in industry. It is extracted through *reduction** by carbon. This reaction takes place in a **blast furnace** using iron ore, coke and limestone (calcium carbonate $CaCO_3$).

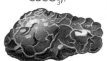

Iron is found in iron oxide called **haematite.**

It has the chemical formula, Fe_2O_3.

Stages in the extraction of iron

1. Hot coke burns to form carbon dioxide: $C(s) + O_2(g) \longrightarrow CO_2(g)$

2. Carbon dioxide is reduced to carbon monoxide: $CO_2(g) + C(s) \longrightarrow 2CO(g)$

3. Carbon monoxide reduces iron oxide: $Fe_2O_3(s) + 3CO(g) \longrightarrow 2Fe(s) + 3CO_2(g)$

4. The calcium carbonate is decomposed by the intense heat of the furnace: $CaCO_3(s) \longrightarrow CaO(s) + CO_2(g)$

5. The calcium oxide (CaO) reacts with sand and clay-like impurities in the ore (such as calcium silicate): $CaO(s) + SiO_2(s) \longrightarrow CaSiO_3(l)$ The reaction removes some of the

A blast furnace

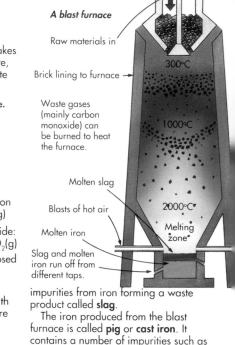

Raw materials in

300°C

Brick lining to furnace

Waste gases (mainly carbon monoxide) can be burned to heat the furnace.

1000°C

Molten slag

Blasts of hot air

2000°C

Melting zone*

Molten iron

Slag and molten iron run off from different taps.

impurities from iron forming a waste product called **slag**.

The iron produced from the blast furnace is called **pig** or **cast iron**. It contains a number of impurities such as carbon, sulphur and silicon.

Steel

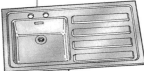

Stainless steel contains nickel and chromium and does not corrode.

Steel, an *alloy** of iron and carbon, is the most commonly used alloy in industry. It is made by blowing oxygen onto molten scrap and pig iron at high pressure. This process removes impurities from the metal in the form of slag and gases. The gases are burned off at high temperature. Various other materials are then added to the iron in order to make different types of steel. For example, mild steel, which contains 0.3% carbon and is very *malleable**, is used in making vehicle bodies.

Aluminium

Aluminium[†] is the most abundant metal in the world, but it is never found in its pure state. It is always combined with other elements in *ores**. Aluminium cannot be extracted by simple reduction in the way that iron can. This is because it is very reactive and forms very strong bonds with oxygen. Instead it has to be extracted by *electrolysis**.

Aluminium is quite high in the reactivity

series but, due to the limited way it *corrodes**, it is stable enough to be used in the manufacture of many household goods.

Aluminium is now used for most of the world's drinks cans.

**Reduction, 18; Alloy, 15; Malleable, 14; Ores, 14; Electrolysis, 22; Corrodes, 24.*
[†]*(Aluminum in US)*

Limestone

Limestone is mainly calcium carbonate ($CaCO_3$). It is a solid found in nature as hard rock and has a number of uses in industry, as shown below.

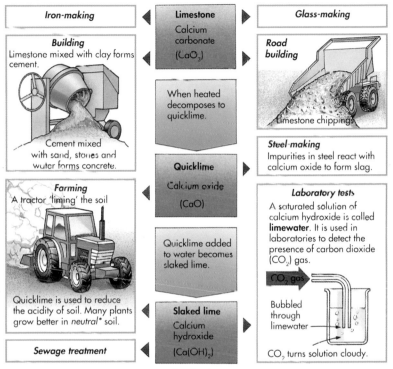

Iron-making

Building
Limestone mixed with clay forms cement.

Cement mixed with sand, stones and water forms concrete.

Farming
A tractor 'liming' the soil

Quicklime is used to reduce the acidity of soil. Many plants grow better in *neutral** soil.

Sewage treatment

Limestone
Calcium carbonate
($CaCO_3$)

When heated decomposes to quicklime.

Quicklime
Calcium oxide
(CaO)

Quicklime added to water becomes slaked lime.

Slaked lime
Calcium hydroxide
($Ca(OH)_2$)

Glass-making

Road building

Limestone chippings

Steel-making
Impurities in steel react with calcium oxide to form slag.

Laboratory tests
A saturated solution of calcium hydroxide is called **limewater**. It is used in laboratories to detect the presence of carbon dioxide (CO_2) gas.

CO_2 gas

Bubbled through limewater

CO_2 turns solution cloudy.

Percentage composition calculations

Resources are often extracted from ores. In industry, it is important to know how much ore is needed to obtain a certain amount of a resource. The method used involves finding what percentage of the ore is made up by the resource. It is called a **percentage composition calculation** and has three stages.

1. Find the relative atomic or molecular mass of the resource.

2. Find the relative molecular mass of the ore and the percentage of ore that is made up of the resource.

3. Divide 100 by the percentage of the resource and then multiply this figure by the amount of the resource required.

This example shows how much iron ore (Fe_2O_3) is needed to make 150 tonnes of iron. The relative atomic mass of iron is 56, and that of oxygen is 16.

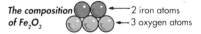

The composition of Fe_2O_3 — 2 iron atoms — 3 oxygen atoms

$(2 \times 56) + (3 \times 16) = 170$
Relative molecular mass = 170

112 parts out of 170 are iron
$112/170 \times 100 = 65.9\%$
65.9% of haematite is iron

150 tonnes of iron required

$$\frac{100}{65.9} \times 150 = 227.6 \text{ tonnes of ore}$$

*Neutral, 25; Relative molecular mass, 7.

Electrolysis

All metals conduct electricity because their structures contain *a sea of electrons** which can move through the metal. If a power supply is connected it acts like a pump causing electrons to flow through the metal. No chemical change occurs when this happens.

Some substances do not conduct electricity when they are in a solid state, but do so when they are melted or dissolved. These substances are called **electrolytes**. When electricity is passed through an electrolyte, a chemical change occurs. The electrolyte breaks up into *ions** which conduct the electric current. When an electrolyte conducts electricity, the process is known as **electrolysis**.

*Covalent** substances are not made up of ions; they cannot conduct electricity.

Electrolytic cells

The apparatus used in electrolysis is called an **electrolytic cell**. It consists of an electrolyte, a power supply and two electrically conductive pieces of metal or graphite called **electrodes**. The electrodes are connected to the power supply and are dipped into the electrolyte. Some electrodes used in industry (see opposite page) change chemically during electrolysis. Electrodes that do not change are called **inert electrodes**.

An electrolytic cell

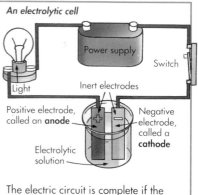

Positive electrode, called an **anode**
Negative electrode, called a **cathode**
Inert electrodes
Electrolytic solution
Power supply
Switch
Light

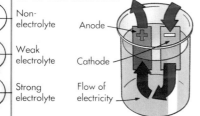

Non-electrolyte
Weak electrolyte
Strong electrolyte
Anode
Cathode
Flow of electricity

The electric circuit is complete if the bulb in an electrolytic cell lights up when connected to the power supply. Electricity is flowing between the annode and the cathode, which means the liquid can conduct electricity and is therefore an electrolyte.

The electrolysis of copper chloride

When a current from a power supply is passed through a solution of copper chloride ($CuCl_2$), chlorine gas and copper are produced. The copper is deposited on one of the electrodes. This happens because copper chloride is an electrolyte which breaks up into copper ions (Cu^{2+}) and chloride ions (Cl^-).

Opposite charges attract, so the positively-charged Cu^{2+} ion is attracted to the negatively-charged cathode, while the negatively-charged Cl^- ion is attracted to the positively-charged anode. When each Cl^- ion arrives at the anode, it gives up one electron. When each Cu^{2+} ion arrives at the cathode, it receives two electrons. These processes can be shown by *ionic equations** like the ones below:

$$Cu^{2+}(aq) + 2e^- \longrightarrow Cu(s)$$
$$2Cl^-(aq) \longrightarrow 2Cl(g) + 2e^-$$

Single chlorine atoms combine in pairs whenever possible, each producing a molecule of chlorine gas (Cl_2).

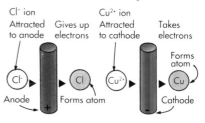

Cl^- ion
Attracted to anode
Gives up electrons
Anode
Forms atom

Cu^{2+} ion
Attracted to cathode
Takes electrons
Forms atom
Cathode

*Sea of electrons, 13; Ions, 12; Covalent, 13; Ionic equations, 12.

Electrolysis of aqueous solutions

Water always contains some molecules which have split into *hydroxide** (OH⁻) and hydrogen (H⁺) ions. These ions undergo changes during the electrolysis of an *aqueous solution**. The OH⁻ ions move to the anode where oxygen gas is produced. The H⁺ ions move to the cathode where hydrogen gas is produced. This is shown in the following equation.

$$2H^+(aq) + 2e^- \longrightarrow H_2(g)$$
$$2OH^-(aq) \longrightarrow H_2O(l) + \tfrac{1}{2}O_2(g) + 2e^-$$

These gases are produced along with the products from the electrolyte.

Electrolysis and its products

Substance electrolysed	At anode	At cathode
Hydrochloric acid	Chlorine	Hydrogen
Sodium chloride	Chlorine	Hydrogen
Molten lead bromide	Bromine	Lead
Aqueous potassium iodide	Iodine	Hydrogen
Copper(II) sulphate (inert electrodes)	Oxygen	Copper
Copper(II) sulphate (copper electrodes)	Anode dissolves	Copper
Aluminium oxide	Oxygen	Aluminium

The table shows the products created by the electrolysis of certain compounds. As a general rule, metals and/or hydrogen are discharged at the cathode and non-metals and/or oxygen are discharged at the anode.

Industrial uses of electrolysis

Electrolysis is used in a number of industrial processes involving metals.

Many metals can be industrially extracted from their *ores** by electrolysis. Aluminium's main ore, bauxite, consists mainly of aluminium oxide. The extraction of aluminium uses large amounts of electricity. For this reason aluminium plants are often close to a source of cheap electricity, such as a hydro-electric dam.

Aluminium oxide has a very high melting point (over 2000°C.) but it can be dissolved in a solution containing molten *cryolite** at a much lower temperature. Electrolysis is then performed in a special tank with a carbon lining that acts as a cathode.

At the cathode: $Al^{3+} + 3e^- \longrightarrow Al$
At the anode: $2O^- - 4e^- \longrightarrow O_2$

Electrolysis can be used to *purify** metals. For example, if impure copper is used as an anode and placed in a solution of copper sulphate ($CuSO_4$), the copper dissolves and is deposited on the cathode, leaving behind the impurities.

The purification of copper

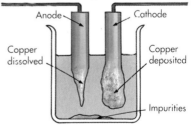

Anode — Cathode
Copper dissolved
Copper deposited
Impurities

Copper sulphate solution

Electroplating is a technique used for plating objects in metal. The object is used as a non-inert electrode and coated with a thin layer of a substance from the electrolyte. For example, if a nail is suspended in copper(II) sulphate solution, it will become plated in copper. In industry, chromium-plated iron is used to make bicycle and car parts.

Aluminium extraction
— Carbon anodes
Carbon-lined steel vessel as cathode
Aluminium collects near cathode.
Aluminium tapped off

*Hydroxide, 58; Aqueous solution, 58 ; Ores, 14; Cryolite, 58; Purify (purity), 5.

23

Corrosion

When a metal reacts with the oxygen in air (usually in the presence of water), it is undergoing **corrosion**. First, the metal loses its lustre or shine, then the structure of the metal breaks down. Corrosion is a slow process. Metals high in the reactivity series, such as sodium, magnesium and calcium, corrode more easily. Lead, which is near the bottom of the reactivity series, is resistant to corrosion and was once used for roofing. Metals at the bottom of the reactivity series, such as gold and silver, hardly corrode at all.

Corrosion can be very serious as it makes metal objects unusable.

Rusting of iron and steel

The corrosion of iron and steel is known as **rusting**. Rusting involves a reaction between the metal, oxygen in the air and water. This can be shown in the following experiment in which iron nails are put into three test tubes. The first test tube contains air and water, the second only water, and the third, air but no water.

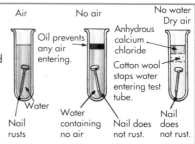

Air / No air / No water Dry air

Oil prevents any air entering.

Anhydrous calcium chloride

Cotton wool stops water entering test tube.

Water

Nail rusts

Water containing no air

Nail does not rust.

Nail does not rust.

Protection of iron and steel

Iron and steel can be protected from corrosion in a number of different ways.

Greasing is used for moving parts but the grease has to be renewed regularly.

Painting is used for large objects but needs to be reapplied when the paint surface is broken.

Galvanizing involves coating steel with a layer of zinc, which is more reactive than steel. If the surface is scratched, the oxygen reacts with the zinc rather than the steel.

Tin-plating is used on cans to prevent corrosion. However, tin is less reactive than steel and if the outer surface of tin is scratched through, the steel underneath will corrode.

Chromium-plating is performed by electrolysis and forms a brightly shining surface. It is used for decoration as well as protection.

The iron hulls of ships can be protected by attaching bars of a more reactive metal such as zinc, to the iron. This metal corrodes first and is called a **sacrificial metal**.

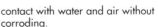

Zinc bars

Corrosion of aluminium

Aluminium reacts rapidly with the oxygen in air to create aluminium oxide. This forms a tough layer on the metal's outer surface, preventing any further reaction with air and water. This explains why household products made from aluminium, such as saucepans and kitchen foil, can come into regular contact with water and air without corroding.

The aluminium oxide layer can be thickened by being used as the *anode** in a form of *electrolysis** known as anodizing. This protects the aluminium further and allows the outer surface to be painted and decorated.

Acids, bases and salts

Acids are compounds which contain the hydrogen *ion** H+ and dissolve in water. Examples of acids include hydrochloric acid (HCl), sulphuric acid (H_2SO_4) and ethanoic acid (CH_3COOH). Acids are *electrolytes** and the acids found in foodstuffs (like the citric acid in lemons) taste sour and sharp. Many acids are highly *corrosive** and have warning labels on their containers. A list of hazard labels can be found on page 47.

Hazard label for corrosive substances

Bases and alkalis

Bases are substances which can accept acids' hydrogen ions. The oxide ion in metal oxides (O^{2-}) and the hydroxide ion in metal hydroxides (OH^-) are both able to combine with the H+ ion. Therefore all metal oxides and hydroxides, such as sodium hydroxide (NaOH) and magnesium oxide (MgO), are bases. Many bases have a soapy feel. A base that is soluble in water is called an **alkali**.

There are three common alkalis.

Sodium hydroxide (NaOH)

Potassium hydroxide (KOH)

Ammonia solution (NH_3(aq))

Ammonia gas bubbled through water creates a solution of positive ammonium ions and negative hydroxide ions.
$$NH_3(g) + H_2O(l) \longrightarrow NH_4^+(aq) + OH^-(aq)$$

Proton donors and acceptors

Acids

Vinegar

Citrus fruits

A hydrogen ion is a hydrogen atom which has lost its electron and now consists of just one proton. An acid contains many protons, and seeks to lose them in reactions. Acids, therefore, are said to be **proton donors**. A base, on the other hand will accept hydrogen ions. Bases are referred to as **proton acceptors**.

Bases

Household cleaner

Bicarbonate of soda

Indigestion tablets

Indicators and the pH number

The **pH number** of a substance tells you how acidic or alkaline the substance is. It stands for the 'power of hydrogen' and is a measure of the concentration of hydrogen ions in a solution. pH values are found on a scale generally between 0 and 14. The lower the pH number, the greater the concentration of hydrogen ions and the more acidic the substance. pH 7 is neutral. A substance with a pH value of above 7 is a base. For example, lemon juice has a pH of 2.1 and is acidic, whereas household ammonia, an alkali, has a pH value of 11.9.

The pH number is determined by an **indicator**, a substance whose colour changes when the pH changes. There are a number of different indicators. **Litmus indicator** distinguishes solely between an acid (which turns it red) and an alkali (which turns it blue). With **universal indicators** the colour varies according to the pH scale.

pH scale

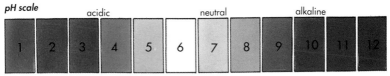

acidic   neutral   alkaline

1 2 3 4 5 6 7 8 9 10 11 12

Ion, 12; Electrolytes, 22; Corrosive, 24.

25

Strong and weak acids and bases

The concentration of an acidic or basic solution may vary, but the strength of the acid or base is constant. The strength of an acid or base is determined by its ability to *ionize**, that is, the ability of its *cations** and *anions** to split up. For example, hydrochloric acid, which is strong, can completely ionize all its hydrogen atoms in water. Similarly, a

strong base, such as sodium hydroxide, can ionize all its hydroxide atoms.

Weak acids, like ethanoic acid, can only partially ionize; only a small number of their molecules split to form hydrogen ions. Similarly, only a small number of molecules of weak bases, such as calcium hydroxide, split up to produce hydroxide ions.

Strong acid

$$HCl(aq) \rightleftharpoons H^+(aq) + Cl^-(aq)$$

Weak acid

$$CH_3COOH(aq) \rightleftharpoons CH_3COO^-(aq) + H^+(aq)$$

Cl⁻   H⁺ The molecules all split up.

Reversible reaction* symbol
The heavier arrow shows the direction the reaction tends to go.

Some molecules split up.

CH_3COO^- H⁺

Neutralization

When an acid and a base are mixed together they form an ionic compound called a **salt**. If excess acid or base is added, the final solution will contain water, a salt and some of the excess acid or base. A chemical reaction between an acid and a base, in which all of the acid and base are completely used up, is called **neutralizaton**. A salt and water are produced and the

resulting solution is usually neutral.

Neutralization reactions occur frequently in everyday life, for example in *liming** the soil and in relieving indigestion caused by too much stomach acid.

Bee stings are acidic. Acid can be neutralized and the sting soothed by applying an alkali.

Reactions of acids and bases

1. Acids react with metals above copper in the *reactivity series**, to form salts and hydrogen. For example:

$$2HCl + Mg \longrightarrow MgCl_2 + H_2$$
Hydrochloric acid / Magnesium / Magnesium chloride

2. Metal hydroxides and metal oxides, such as copper oxide, react in the same way as metals, producing a salt and water.

$$CuO + 2HCl \longrightarrow CuCl_2 + H_2O$$
Copper oxide / Hydrochloric acid / Copper chloride / Water

3. Metal carbonates and metal hydrogen carbonates are similar to bases. They react with acids to form a salt and water, but they also produce carbon dioxide.

$$Na_2CO_3 + 2HNO_3 \longrightarrow 2NaNO_3 + CO_2 + H_2O$$
Sodium carbonate / Nitric acid / Sodium nitrate / Carbon dioxide

4. When in solution, the salts of some metals, such as magnesium, often react with the hydroxide (OH⁻) ions in an alkali to form an insoluble metal hydroxide.

5. When a base is warmed with an ammonium compound, ammonia gas is produced. For example, ammonium chloride and calcium hydroxide produce calcium chloride and ammonia. This reaction is used to make ammonia gas, and as a test to see whether a substance is an ammonium compound.

Preparation of salts

There are a number of ways in which salts can be prepared in the laboratory. Direct combination is one method, but it can only be used when the salt consists of two elements. For example, the salt iron sulphide is made by direct combination when iron and sulphur are heated together.

Making a soluble salt

A soluble salt can be made by the reaction between an acid and an insoluble metal or an insoluble base.

For example, copper sulphate can be made from sulphuric acid and copper as shown below.

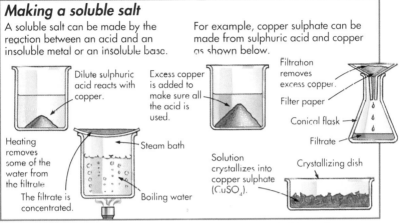

Dilute sulphuric acid reacts with copper.

Excess copper is added to make sure all the acid is used.

Filtration removes excess copper.

Filter paper

Conical flask

Filtrate

Heating removes some of the water from the filtrate.

Steam bath

The filtrate is concentrated.

Boiling water

Solution crystallizes into copper sulphate ($CuSO_4$).

Crystallizing dish

Titration

An alkali will neutralize an acid but, because the salt produced is soluble, it cannot be separated by filtration. A *titration** will determine the exact volumes needed for neutralization without the use of an indicator. The process can then be repeated and the salt can then be isolated by evaporation. For example, if a titration is used to combine the correct quantities of sodium hydroxide and hydrochloric acid, it will produce the salt sodium chloride.

Making insoluble salts

Two soluble substances are needed to form an insoluble salt. For example, to form the insoluble salt lead chloride, you need a soluble compound of lead (lead nitrate, for instance) and a soluble chloride (such as sodium chloride).

$$Pb(NO_3)_2 + 2NaCl \rightarrow PbCl_2 + 2NaNO_3$$
Lead nitrate | Sodium chloride | Lead chloride | Sodium nitrate

Lead chloride is the one insoluble product. It forms a *precipitate** which can be isolated by *filtration**.

Choosing a method of making a salt

It is important to know which method of preparation is correct for each type of salt. Instead of learning a long list of salts and appropriate methods, it is easier to ask a series of questions about the salt and its components. These questions are shown in the diagram opposite.

Analysis of salts can be found on page 52.

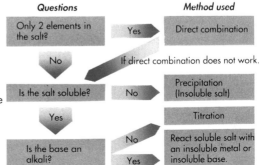

Questions		Method used
Only 2 elements in the salt?	Yes	Direct combination
No		If direct combination does not work.
Is the salt soluble?	No	Precipitation (Insoluble salt)
Yes		Titration
Is the base an alkali?	No	React soluble salt with an insoluble metal or insoluble base.
	Yes	

*Titration, 51; Precipitate, 59; Filtration, 50.

The mole

Although atoms are too small to count individually, chemists need to know how many are present in a sample. To do this, they use a set number of particles as a base unit of measurement. This unit is called a **mole**. The number of atoms in a mole is the number of atoms found in 12g of carbon-12, which is 6 x 10^{23} (600,000 billion billion[†]). This is called the **Avogadro number**.

$$6 \times 10^{23}$$

This equals 23 zeros following the 6.

$$= 600,000,000,000$$
$$000,000,000,000$$

Calculations of reacting mass

A calculation to determine how much of a substance is used in a reaction is called a calculation of **reacting mass**.

All substances in a reaction are in ratio to one another. For example, the ratio of hydrogen and oxygen atoms in water is 2:1. Knowing the ratios and the amount

The mass, in grammes, of a mole of any element is equal to that element's *relative atomic mass**. The mass, in grammes, of a mole of a compound is that compound's *relative molecular mass**. A mole of two different substances will have the same number of particles but, as they have different relative atomic masses, they will weigh different amounts.

1 mole of magnesium: 24g

1 mole of carbon: 12g

of a product or reagent used, you can calculate in three stages how much of the other substances is used and created. In the example below, the amounts of the other substances can be found if you know that 10g of sodium hydroxide is used.

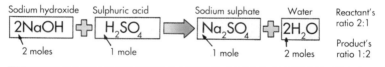

Sodium hydroxide — Sulphuric acid

| 2NaOH | ⊕ | H₂SO₄ |

2 moles — 1 mole

Sodium sulphate — Water

| Na₂SO₄ | ⊕ | 2H₂O |

1 mole — 2 moles

Reactant's ratio 2:1

Product's ratio 1:2

To determine how many grammes there are in a mole of each substance, find the relative molecular mass of each substance. This figure is equal to the number of grammes in a mole.

Substance	Relative molecular mass
Sodium hydroxide	40
Sulphuric acid	98
Sodium sulphate	142
Water	18

Find out how many moles of the substance of known weight are used in the reaction. In the example, a mole of sodium hydroxide has a mass of 40g, so 10g equals ¹/₄ mole. Using the ratios

between the products and reactants you can then calculate how many moles of the other substance are involved in the reaction. In the example, the amounts of the other substances are shown below.

| 2NaOH | ⊕ | H₂SO₄ | ➡ | Na₂SO₄ | ⊕ | 2H₂O |

¹/₄ mole — ¹/₈ mole — ¹/₈ mole — ¹/₄ mole

Multiply the number of moles used by the weight of a mole of each substance.
¹/₈ mole sulphuric acid (98g) = 12.25g
¹/₈ mole sodium sulphate (142g) = 17.75g

¹/₄ mole water (18g) = 4.5g
There should be an equal mass of substances on each side of the equation. In the example, there are 22.5g of both reactants and products.

*Relative atomic mass, 7; Relative molecular mass, 7.
[†]Billion = thousand million.

Calculating the formula of a compound

Chemists can calculate the formula of a compound if they know how much of each substance is used to create it. The unknown substance in the example below is made from 2.34g of Potassium (K) and 0.96g of Sulphur (S). Its formula can be determined by finding the mass of a mole of each substance and then finding the number of moles of each substance in the compound.

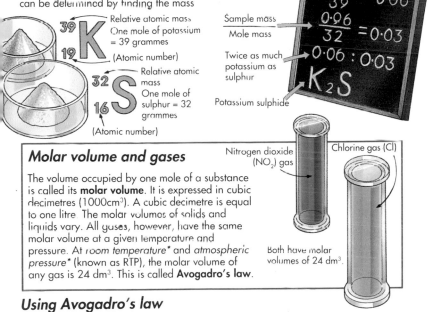

Relative atomic mass
One mole of potassium = 39 grammes
(Atomic number)

Relative atomic mass
One mole of sulphur = 32 grammes
(Atomic number)

Sample mass
Mole mass

$\frac{2.34}{39} = 0.06$

Sample mass
Mole mass

$\frac{0.96}{32} = 0.03$

Twice as much potassium as sulphur

$0.06 : 0.03$

K_2S

Potassium sulphide

Molar volume and gases

The volume occupied by one mole of a substance is called its **molar volume**. It is expressed in cubic decimetres ($1000cm^3$). A cubic decimetre is equal to one litre. The molar volumes of solids and liquids vary. All gases, however, have the same molar volume at a given temperature and pressure. At *room temperature** and *atmospheric pressure** (known as RTP), the molar volume of any gas is 24 dm³. This is called **Avogadro's law**.

Nitrogen dioxide (NO_2) gas

Chlorine gas (Cl)

Both have molar volumes of 24 dm³.

Using Avogadro's law

Avogadro's law is useful for finding out how much of a gas is used in an equation. The reaction below shows the decomposition of potassium hydrogencarbonate, which produces carbon dioxide gas. If you know how many grammes of potassium hydrogencarbonate are used (in this case, 20g), you can find the volume of carbon dioxide produced.

1. Find the mass of one mole of potassium hydrogencarbonate (This is the same as its relative molecular mass: 100g.) Then calculate the ratio in moles between the substances involved in the reaction.

$2KHCO_3 \Rightarrow K_2CO_3 + H_2O + CO_2$

2 moles   1 mole

Two moles (200g) of potassium hydrogencarbonate produce one mole of carbon dioxide.

2. Calculate how many moles of carbon dioxide are produced when 20g of potassium hydrogencarbonate are used: 20g/200g = ¹/₁₀. This means that a reaction involving 20g of potassium hydrogencarbonate produces ¹/₁₀ mole of carbon dioxide. As one mole of CO_2 occupies 24 litres at RTP, this reaction produces 2.4 litres of carbon dioxide.

*Room temperature, 5; Atmospheric pressure, 5.

Water

Water is essential to life. Your body needs approximately two litres of liquids each day but each person uses many times that. Flushing the toilet uses 10 litres of water, and a bath can take as much as 70 litres.

In industry, millions of litres are used for cooling, washing and as a *solvent**. For example, it takes 10 litres of water to make 1 litre of lemonade, 50,000 litres to make one car, and 5 million litres to cool a power station each day.

Water is sometimes known as the **universal solvent**. This is because a large number of substances can be dissolved to some extent in water. Because of its solvent properties, natural supplies of water contain many impurities. Water free of impurities is called **distilled water**.

The water cycle

Water in the atmosphere *condenses** in the air and falls to earth as rain or snow. Warmed by the sun, water evaporates back into the atmosphere. This process is called the **water cycle**.

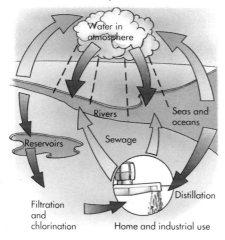

Water in atmosphere

Rivers

Seas and oceans

Reservoirs

Sewage

Distillation

Filtration and chlorination

Home and industrial use

Water purification

Clean water is essential for healthy living. Certain impurities in water can be harmful to animals and humans and can spread diseases such as cholera. In order to prevent this, the water that reaches your tap has been through two processes. The first, **filtration**, is designed to remove solid particles from the water. Screens remove pieces of rubbish and settling tanks remove smaller particles. In the second process, **chlorination**, chlorine is added to the water to kill bacteria. In some countries, fluoride is also added to protect teeth from decay.

Waste water and materials are called **sewage**. At one time, all sewage was piped back into rivers and seas, causing a lot of disease. In some places this is still done, but in most the sewage is treated first. It is mixed with air and decomposed by bacteria into harmless products.

Settling tank
Solid particles drop to bottom.

Detergents

Detergents are substances which when added to water enable it to remove dirt. Detergents do this in three ways. They lower the water's *surface tension**, they enable grease molecules to dissolve in water, and they keep the removed dirt in *suspension** in the water. Soaps are one type of detergent, but there are many soapless detergents as well. The head of a detergent molecule is attracted to water; it is described as **hydrophillic**. The tail of the molecule is **hydrophobic**; it is repelled by water.

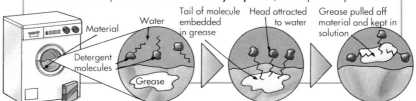

Material

Water

Detergent molecules

Grease

Tail of molecule embedded in grease

Head attracted to water

Grease pulled off material and kept in solution

*Solvent, 50; Condenses, 5; Surface tension, 59; Suspension, 50.

Water pollution

Polluted water contains either too little oxygen or too many toxic substances and can support little or no life.

Untreated sewage, fertilizers, oil, detergents and industrial waste are the most common causes of water pollution.

Rain washes fertilizers from fields into rivers and lakes.

Industrial waste, such as heavy metals* and acids, are poisonous.

Non-biodegradable* foam from detergents stop oxygen from entering the water. Aquatic life dies.

Fertilizers contain substances called nitrates* and phosphates*. These stimulate excessive growth of bacteria and water plants, which use up all the oxygen in the water and die. Oxygen dissolved in water is vital to aquatic life. Once the oxygen is gone, fish and other aquatic creatures die too. This process is called **eutrophication**.

Oil pollution of water

Detergent is used to break up oil slicks.

Oil forms a film on the surface of water restricting the entry of sunlight. This prevents the oxidizing* bacteria and small organisms from breeding and living. The creatures die and this adversely affects the food web*.

Most oil pollution occurs at sea, partly from oil tanker accidents, but mainly from the dumping of waste oil from tankers and refineries. This oil pollutes beaches and kills birds and fish.

Hard water

Water containing a lot of calcium and magnesium salts* is called **permanent hard water**. Water containing a lot of the salt calcium hydrogencarbonate is called **temporary hard water**. These salts have some benefits. For example, calcium helps maintain healthy teeth and gums. However, hard water is considered a nuisance. It does not easily produce a lather. The calcium ions* in hard water react with soap forming an insoluble solid called **scum**.

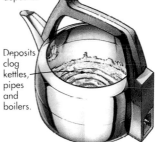

Hard water leaves insoluble deposits.

Deposits clog kettles, pipes and boilers.

Water softening

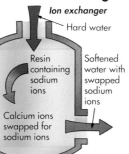

Ion exchanger

Hard water

Resin containing sodium ions

Softened water with swapped sodium ions

Calcium ions swapped for sodium ions

Temporary hard water can be softened by boiling. Permanent hard water can be softened in four ways. The first method, distilling*, uses a lot of energy and is too expensive for household use. Another way is to use enough soap to react with all the calcium ions, but this wastes soap and creates a lot of scum.

However, there are two more practical methods. Sodium carbonate (known as washing soda) can be added to remove calcium ions by forming calcium carbonate: $(Ca^{2+}(aq) + CO_3^{2-}(aq) \longrightarrow CaCO_3(s))$. The second method swaps the damaging calcium ions for sodium ions which do not form scum. This is known as **ion exchange**.

*Heavy metals, 58; Non-biodegradable, 44; Nitrates, 37; Phosphates, 59; Oxidizing, 18; Food web, 58; Salts, 26; Ions, 12; Distilling (Distillation), 50.

Energy changes

The capacity to work is called **energy**. Heat, light, electricity and chemical energy are all different types of energy. In most chemical reactions, energy (usually in the form of heat) is either given out or taken in. If a chemical reaction produces heat, it is said to be an **exothermic** reaction. If heat is taken in from the surroundings, it is called an **endothermic** reaction.

Exothermic reactions

Respiration*, *neutralization** and many reactions which involve the formation of bonds between atoms and molecules are all exothermic.

Combustion* is also exothermic. This can be seen in the following experiment. Ethanol is burned in a spirit burner with a beaker of water placed on a tripod above the burner. The temperature of the water can be observed to rise. This is due to the heat given out by the combustion reaction.

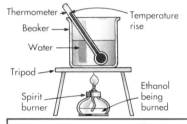

Endothermic reactions

Most reactions which result in the breaking of bonds between atoms and molecules draw in heat energy and are therefore endothermic. Endothermic reactions include *photosynthesis** and *electrolysis**.

Another type of endothermic reaction occurs when ammonium chloride crystals are dissolved in water. This is shown in the experiment below.

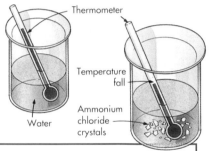

Measuring energy changes

Energy is measured in units called **joules**. 1000 joules equals a **kilojoule** (or **kJ** for short). It can be important to know how much energy is required to raise the temperature of a substance. The amount of energy in joules needed to raise the temperature of one gram of a substance by one *Kelvin** (or K) is known as the **specific heat capacity**. This figure varies according to the substance. The specific heat capacity of water, for example, is 4.2 joules per gram per K. (A Kelvin is equal to one degree Celsius).

Diagrams which show energy changes in terms of the energy levels of the *reagents** and *products** in a reaction are called **energy level diagrams**. The difference in energy between the reagents and the products is known as the **enthalpy change**.

The enthalpy change is measured in units of kilojoules per *mole**, or **kJmol⁻¹** for short. The symbol for enthalpy change is a triangle followed by a capital H: ΔH or delta H. The example below shows the energy level diagram for the formation of the gas methane:

$$\boxed{C} \quad + \quad \boxed{2H_2} \quad \Rightarrow \quad \boxed{CH_4}$$

Energy level diagram

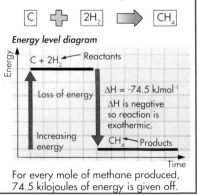

For every mole of methane produced, 74.5 kilojoules of energy is given off.

Direction of energy change

If a chemical reaction is exothermic in one direction, then the reverse reaction will be endothermic. This is shown on an energy level diagram by the direction of the arrow representing the enthalpy change ΔH. For example, when carbon is oxidized to form carbon dioxide ($C + O_2 \longrightarrow CO_2$), the enthalpy change is negative (the energy level decreases). For the reverse reaction, it is positive.

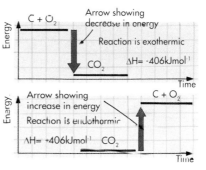

Arrow showing decrease in energy

Reaction is exothermic

$C + O_2$

CO_2 $\Delta H = -406kJmol^{-1}$

Arrow showing increase in energy

Reaction is endothermic

$\Delta H = +406kJmol^{-1}$ CO_2

$C + O_2$

Calculating energy changes

It is possible to calculate the energy changes in a reaction. You need to know the amounts of substances involved in the reaction and the rise or fall in temperature. For example, from the experiment opposite showing the burning of ethanol, it is found that 0.1g of ethanol raises the temperature of 50g of water by 11K. The specific heat capacity of 50g of water is:

Amount of water **X** Specific heat capacity **=** Joules

If 210 joules of energy are needed to raise 50g of water by 1K, raising the temperature by 11K requires:
$210 \times 11 = 2310J$ or $2.31kJ$.

As energy change is measured in $kJmol^{-1}$ units, you need to know the equivalent of 0.1g of ethanol in moles. A mole of ethanol has a mass of 46g, so 0.1g of ethanol (0.1 divided by 46) equals 0.0022 moles.

If 0.0022 moles of ethanol produces 2.31 kJ of heat energy, then one mole of ethanol will produce:

$$\frac{1}{0.0022} \times 2.31 \text{ kJ} = 1050 \text{ kJmol}^{-1}$$

Activation energy

For a reaction to take place reagent molecules must collide with one another. When they do so they must possess enough energy to cause or initiate a reaction. The level of energy needed to start a reaction is called its **energy barrier**. The actual energy required to start the reaction is called the **activation energy**.

Energy level diagram showing activation energy

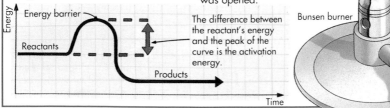

Energy barrier

Reactants

Products

The difference between the reactant's energy and the peak of the curve is the activation energy.

Activation energy is essential to the start of a reaction. For example, in the process of combustion, the activation energy is usually provided by a spark or a flame. This is why a spark from, for example, a lit splint is needed to light a bunsen burner. If no activation energy was needed to start combustion, the gas from the bunsen burner would burn as soon as the gas tap was opened.

Bunsen burner

Rates of reaction

The **rate of reaction** is the rate at which *products** are formed or *reactants** used up in a chemical reaction. The rate of reaction varies greatly. Some chemical reactions, such as explosions, happen very rapidly. Others, like *rusting**, occur very slowly. The rate of a reaction can be affected by a number of factors: temperature, concentration and pressure, *catalyst**, surface area/particle size and light. These are considered below.

Many reaction rates can be measured using the formula:

$$\text{Rate} = \frac{\text{change in amount of a substance}}{\text{time taken}}$$

Readings can be taken and the results plotted to form a **rate curve**. The rate of reaction measured at any one point on the rate curve is called an **instantaneous rate**. In the experiment below, calcium carbonate and hydrochloric acid are reacted together to produce calcium chloride, water and carbon dioxide.

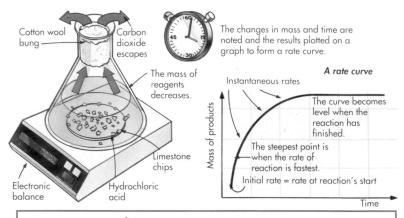

Cotton wool bung

Carbon dioxide escapes

The mass of reagents decreases.

Limestone chips

Electronic balance

Hydrochloric acid

The changes in mass and time are noted and the results plotted on a graph to form a rate curve.

A rate curve

Instantaneous rates

Mass of products

The curve becomes level when the reaction has finished.

The steepest point is when the rate of reaction is fastest.

Initial rate = rate at reaction's start

Time

Temperature and reaction rates

The rate of reaction can be affected by temperature. For example, if the above reaction was repeated, but with the reactants heated, the rate curve would be different from the previous one. The change occurs because an increase in temperature increases the speed of most reactions.

The higher the temperature, the more rapidly the particles move. They collide together more frequently and with greater energy.

Particles in a reaction

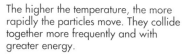

Temperature raised

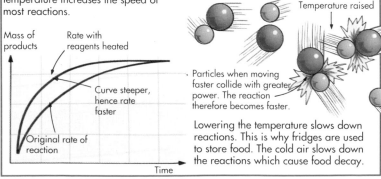

Mass of products

Rate with reagents heated

Curve steeper, hence rate faster

Original rate of reaction

Time

Particles when moving faster collide with greater power. The reaction therefore becomes faster.

Lowering the temperature slows down reactions. This is why fridges are used to store food. The cold air slows down the reactions which cause food decay.

*Products, 16; Reactants, 16; Rusting, 24; Catalyst,35.

Concentration and pressure

The number of reactant particles dissolved in a certain volume of *solvent** is called the **concentration** of a solution. The greater the concentration, the faster the rate of reaction. This is because the particles are closer together and therefore collide more frequently.

With a gas, the rate of reaction is affected by pressure in the same way

that, in a solution, it is affected by concentration. At higher pressures, the reagent gas molecules are forced closer together. This means they are more likely to collide and bring about a reaction. The technique of compressing or concentrating gas is used, for example, in the *Haber Process** for making ammonia.

Catalysts

Catalysts are substances which are added to change the rate of reaction, but are not themselves chemically changed. Many catalysts are used in industry to speed up reactions and lower the cost of the eventual products. For example, a compound of vanadium is used as a catalyst in the production of sulphuric acid.

Catalysts which slow down reactions, are called **inhibitors**. The *oxidizing** of food, for example, is slowed down by catalysts called antioxidants.

In the laboratory the decomposition of hydrogen peroxide is used to

prepare oxygen. The decomposition would be very slow, but for the presence of the catalyst manganese(IV) oxide (MnO_2).

$$MnO_2$$
$$2H_2O_2 \Rightarrow 2H_2O \;+\; O_2$$

Catalyst speeds up reaction

Antioxidants prevent crisps from being oxidized and going stale.

Surface area/particle size

A solid will react faster both physically and chemically, if it is broken up into smaller pieces. This is because a reaction can only take place at the surface of a solid. Breaking an object into more pieces increases its surface area, allowing more collisions with other reactants. For example, hydrochloric acid will react faster with powdered limestone than with limestone chippings. Sugar undergoes a physical reaction when dissolved in tea. Granulated sugar will dissolve quicker than sugar lumps.

10g of sugar grains have a greater surface area than a 10g sugar cube.

More collisions per second with boiling water.

Light

Some reactions and their rates are affected by light. These reactions are called **photosensitive**. The most common reaction of this type is *photosynthesis**, which takes place in green plants. It is the process by which carbon dioxide is converted into glucose, oxygen and energy. Light also plays a vital part in photography. It darkens the silver bromide coating on the film in the camera, to form a negative picture.

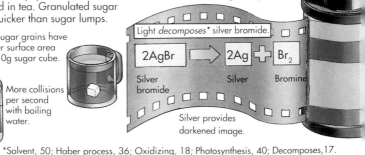

Light *decomposes** silver bromide.

$$2AgBr \Rightarrow 2Ag \;+\; Br_2$$

Silver bromide   Silver   Bromine

Silver provides darkened image.

*Solvent, 50; Haber process, 36; Oxidizing, 18; Photosynthesis, 40; Decomposes, 17.

Nitrogen

Nitrogen is a colourless, odourless gas which makes up 78% of air. It can be isolated from the other gases in air by *fractional distillation**. Nitrogen is used as an unreactive atmosphere for the storage of foods such as crisps and bacon. Ordinary air would *oxidize** the food, turning it stale a lot quicker. Nitrogen does not normally burn and so is used to flush out oil tanks and pipe lines. Liquid nitrogen, with a very low boiling point of -196°C, is used to preserve human organs prior to surgery. It is also used to freeze foods.

The nitrogen cycle

Nitrogen is present in a wide range of compounds in nature. It is an essential element in the making of *proteins** which are needed for growth. Nitrogen is constantly recycled in nature in a process called the **nitrogen cycle**.

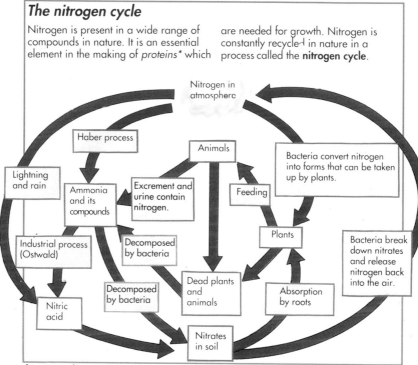

Ammonia

Nitrogen and hydrogen are the elements used to make ammonia (NH_3), a poisonous, colourless gas which has a pungent odour. The method used in industry to make ammonia is called the **Haber Process**. It was invented in 1909 by the German chemist, Fritz Haber. The process operates at a high temperature (approx 450°C) and pressure (*up to 1000 atmospheres**), with iron as a catalyst.

$$N_2(g) + 3H_2(g) \rightleftharpoons 2NH_3(g)$$
Nitrogen Hydrogen   Ammonia

The Haber process is a *reversible reaction**. The gases are cooled and the ammonia is separated. Only about 15% of the mixture is converted to ammonia. The unreacted substances are recycled.

Ammonia forms an *alkaline** solution in water called ammonium hydroxide, or aqueous ammonia.

Aqueous ammonia is a degreasing agent. Household cleaners contain ammonia to cut through grease.

*Fractional distillation, 41; Oxidize, 18; Proteins, 59; Atmospheres, 5; Reversible reaction, 17; Alkaline, 25.

Nitric acid

Nitric acid (HNO_3) is manufactured in a three-stage process called the **Ostwald process**. First, ammonia is oxidized, with the help of a high temperature (900°C) and a platinum-rhodium catalyst, to form nitrogen monoxide:
$$4NH_3(g) + 5O_2(g) \longrightarrow 4NO(g) + 6H_2O(l)$$
The nitrogen monoxide cools and reacts with oxygen to produce nitrogen dioxide:
$$2NO(g) + O_2(g) \longrightarrow 2NO_2(g)$$
Finally, nitrogen dioxide reacts with water and oxygen to produce nitric acid:
$$4NO_2(g) + O_2(g) + 2H_2O(l) \longrightarrow 4HNO_3(l)$$
Nitric acid is used to make many common fertilizers, including ammonium nitrate (NH_4NO_3) as well as other products such as dyes and synthetic fibres. It is a very powerful oxidizing agent. Salts of nitric acid which contain the ion NO_3^- are called **nitrates**. Nitrates are used mainly in the making of fertilizers.

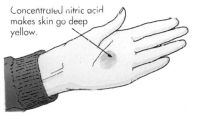

Concentrated nitric acid makes skin go deep yellow.

Fertilizers

Massive increases in population this century have made it necessary to grow more and more crops to keep people alive. This increase has upset the balance of nitrogen and other elements in the soil, which has been maintained for thousands of years. Soils which are continually sown with crops do not get the chance to replace the missing nitrogen. So farmers use chemical fertilizers made from ammonia to replace it. Other elements that have been depleted can also be replaced artificially. However, the overuse of fertilizers can have damaging effects (see below).

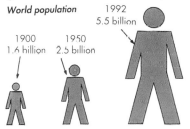

World population

1900
1.6 billion

1950
2.5 billion

1992
5.5 billion

Damaging effects of fertilizer overuse	
The effect	Resulting damage
Changes the soil pH	Plants die, *food web** affected
Unwanted elements accumulate in soil	Eventually poisons soil, plants die
Fertilizer compounds washed into rivers	Causes *eutrophication**
Harms plants and animals in soil	Breaks down food web

NPK values

Most fertilizers are a mixture of compounds containing nitrogen, phosphorous and potassium (the three elements which most need replacement in the soil). These fertilizers are assigned a series of numbers showing the percentage of nitrogen, phosphorous(V) oxide (P_2O_5) and potassium oxide (K_2O) contained in the fertilizer. This number is called the **NPK value**.

NPK Fertilizer

18% N

12% P_2O_5

15% K_2O

18:12:15

SPEEDY GROW

* *Food web, 58; Eutrophication, 31.*

Sulphur and chlorine

Sulphur occurs naturally in volcanic regions in underground deposits known as **sulphur beds**. It is also found in fossil fuels and combined in ores such as copper sulphide (CuS).

Sulphur is a non-metallic, brittle solid which can be powdered. It does not conduct electricity and does not dissolve in water. It is coloured a bright yellow.

Sulphur's most important use is in the making of sulphuric acid (see below). It

Sulphur crystal

is also used in a process called **vulcanization** to make rubber harder and tougher for use in products like tyres and hoses.

When sulphur burns it produces a blue flame and is converted to sulphur dioxide (SO_2). Sulphur dioxide is a poisonous gas. It is a common air pollutant because it is frequently found as an impurity in fossil fuels. However sulphur dioxide also has important uses. It can be used as a *reducing agent**, as a *bleach**, and as a good preservative for food products containing fruit.

Sulphur dioxide is used to kill insects such as cockroaches. This process is called **fumigation**.

Sulphuric acid

The process used to manufacture sulphuric acid (H_2SO_4) is called the **contact process**. First, sulphur is *combusted** to make sulphur dioxide.

$$\boxed{S(s)} \;\boxed{+}\; \boxed{O_2(g)} \;\Rightarrow\; \boxed{SO_2(g)}$$

Then, more oxygen is reacted with the sulphur dioxide to make sulphur trioxide (SO_3). Heat (450°C) and a vanadium(V) oxide (V_2O_5) *catalyst** are used to speed up the process.

$$\boxed{2SO_2(g)} \;\boxed{+}\; \boxed{O_2(g)} \;\Rightarrow\; \boxed{2SO_3(g)}$$

Finally, sulphur trioxide is passed into concentrated sulphuric acid to form fuming sulphuric acid, called **oleum**.

$$\boxed{SO_3(g)} \;\boxed{+}\; \boxed{H_2SO_4(l)} \;\Rightarrow\; \boxed{H_2S_2O_7(l)}$$

Oleum $H_2S_2O_7(l)$ is diluted into concentrated sulphuric acid (H_2SO_4).

Sulphuric acid is known as a **dibasic** acid because it contains two hydrogen atoms which become hydrogen *ions** when dissolved in water. It is very reactive and highly corrosive. Much care needs to be taken in its transportation, handling and storage.

Sulphuric acid produces a large amount of heat when dissolved in water. The acid must always be added to the water and not the other way round. This way, the acid is rapidly diluted and the heat safely absorbed by the water.

Sulphuric acid is stored in special containers.

Hazard signs

Harmful

Corrosive

Sulphuric acid as a dehydrating agent

Concentrated sulphuric acid is described as a good **dehydrating agent**, which means that it absorbs moisture from a number of other substances. For example, a beaker of the acid left open will gradually increase in volume because it absorbs water from the air. When sulphuric acid is added to sugar, it absorbs the water from sugar, leaving carbon as a hot, black mass.

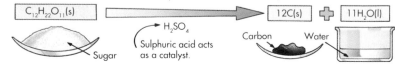

$$\boxed{C_{12}H_{22}O_{11}(s)} \;\Longrightarrow\; \boxed{12C(s)} \;\boxed{+}\; \boxed{11H_2O(l)}$$

Sugar

H_2SO_4
Sulphuric acid acts as a catalyst.

Carbon   Water

*Fossil fuels, 40; Reducing agent, 18; Bleach, 58; Combusted, 10; Catalyst, 35; Ions, 12.

Uses of sulphuric acid

Sulphuric acid is very important industrially. It is commonly used as a raw material in the manufacture of many products, some of which are shown opposite.

Detergents

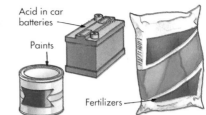
Acid in car batteries
Paints
Fertilizers

Chlorine

Chlorine is a *halogen** found in Group VII of the periodic table. At room temperature it is a greenish-yellow gas which is very poisonous. Chlorine is used to kill bacteria in the water supply. It is also important in the manufacture of paints, aerosol propellants, bleach, disinfectants, insecticides and plastics.

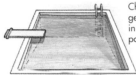
Chlorine kills germs found in swimming pools.

Most compounds formed when chlorine combines with another element are called **chlorides**. Chlorides of non-metals, such as hydrogen chloride, are usually *covalent** compounds. Chlorides of metals, such as magnesium chloride, are usually water soluble *ionic** compounds.

Hydrogen chloride is a colourless gas made by burning hydrogen in chlorine. It reacts with ammonia and dissolves in water to form hydrochloric acid.

Hydrochloric acid

Hydrochloric acid is used in industry for cleaning metals in a process called **pickling**. It is also used in electronics to make printed circuit boards. In the laboratory hydrochloric acid is used with barium chloride to detect the presence of sulphate (SO_4^{2-}) ions in a substance.

Test for sulphate ions using hydrochloric acid

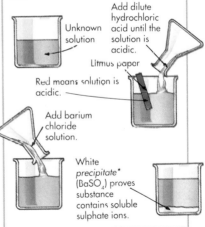

Unknown solution
Add dilute hydrochloric acid until the solution is acidic.

Litmus paper
Red means solution is acidic.

Add barium chloride solution.

White *precipitate** ($BaSO_4$) proves substance contains soluble sulphate ions.

Sodium chloride

Sodium chloride (NaCl) is an ionic compound which readily dissolves in water. It is better known as **common salt**. It can be extracted from sea water and is found in solid form as **rock salt**. Salt is used to flavour and preserve food. It is essential to animal life, although too much in your regular diet can be harmful. Salt is sprinkled on roads in winter to lower the *freezing point** of water and prevent ice forming.

Sodium chloride is also used as a raw material for a number of other important substances. A heavily concentrated solution of sodium chloride is called **brine**. When brine undergoes *electrolysis**, chlorine, hydrogen and sodium hydroxide (a base used in making soaps, detergents and bleaches) can all be extracted.

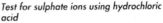

*Halogen, 9; Covalent, 13; Ionic, 12; Precipitate, 59; Freezing point, 5; Electrolysis, 22.

Organic chemistry

Organic chemistry is the study of compounds containing carbon. It is called organic because chemists used to think that these compounds could only be found in living things. Today we know that they are also to be found in many man-made substances, such as *plastics**. Organic molecules are found in medicines, plastics, fuels and food. **Biotechnology**, the exploitation of plant and animal organic material (known as the **biomass**), is increasing in importance and producing many useful new substances.

Organic molecules are made up of carbon atoms bonded together by *covalent bonds**. The simplest organic molecules contain only hydrogen and carbon atoms and are called **hydrocarbons** (HC).

The carbon cycle

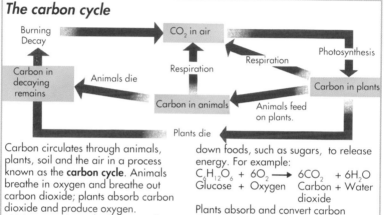

Carbon circulates through animals, plants, soil and the air in a process known as the **carbon cycle**. Animals breathe in oxygen and breathe out carbon dioxide; plants absorb carbon dioxide and produce oxygen.

Living organisms obtain energy from their food by means of a slow form of *combustion** called **respiration**. In respiration, oxygen is used to break down foods, such as sugars, to release energy. For example:

$$C_6H_{12}O_6 + 6O_2 \longrightarrow 6CO_2 + 6H_2O$$
Glucose + Oxygen → Carbon dioxide + Water

Plants absorb and convert carbon dioxide into sugars using sunlight. This process is called **photosynthesis** and is the reverse of respiration.

$$6CO_2 + 6H_2O \longrightarrow C_6H_{12}O_6 + 6O_2$$

Fossil fuels

Gas, coal and oil are all called **fossil fuels**. They are formed from decaying animal and plant matter over many millions of years. They are called fossil fuels because they are formed under pressure in a similar way to fossil formation. When a fossil fuel burns, it releases a lot of heat energy which can then be harnessed to propel vehicles, produce electricity and provide heating for home and industry. However, it may release waste products which cause pollution (see pages 10-11).

Fossil fuels satisfy most of the world's energy needs but they are *non-renewable resources**. Estimates suggest that our coal supply will last for 200-300 years but our oil and gas reserves may only last 50-60 years. In order to conserve fossil fuels, more use should be made of renewable, non-fossil fuels, such as hydro-electric and solar power. These are called **alternative energies**.

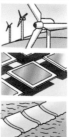

Windmills can harness wind power.

Solar cells convert heat from the sun into electricity.

Tidal barrages exploit energy generated by waves and tides.

*Plastics, 44; Covalent bonds, 13; Combustion, 10; Non-renewable resources, 19.

Oil

Crude oil is a mixture of different organic compounds most of which are hydrocarbons. These hydrocarbons are all different sizes. The smaller ones are lighter and have lower boiling points than the larger molecules. This is because smaller hydrocarbons do not stick together as well as bigger ones.

The hydrocarbons are separated in a process called **refining**. Hydrocarbons which have boiling points within a certain range are grouped together into **fractions**. These fractions are separated from each other in a **fractional distillation column** (also known as a **fractionating tower**). The process starts with the crude oil heated to a temperature of about 350°C. As it boils, the oil vapour passes up the column, losing heat as it rises. The different fractions cool and condense at different places in the column according to their boiling points. Each fraction is separated off and distilled again to make it purer.

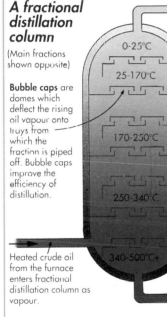

A fractional distillation column

(Main fractions shown opposite)

Bubble caps are domes which deflect the rising oil vapour onto trays from which the fraction is piped off. Bubble caps improve the efficiency of distillation.

Heated crude oil from the furnace enters fractional distillation column as vapour.

0-25°C
25-170°C
170-250°C
250-340°C
340-500°C+

Refinery gas
1-4 carbon atoms in each molecule. Mainly consists of methane. Used for fuels and solvents.

Gasoline (or petrol)
5-10 carbon atoms in each molecule. The fraction most in demand. Used for making other chemicals and as fuel for vehicles.

Kerosene (paraffin)
11-14 carbon atoms in each molecule. Used for fuels in homes and planes.

Diesel oil
15-19 carbon atoms in each molecule. Used as a fuel in diesel engines.

Residue
20-40 carbon atoms in each molecule. This is what is left after fractional distillation. Some is used as heating oil; the rest is re-distilled to form paraffin waxes (used for candles and polishes), lubricating oil and **bitumen** which is used for surfacing roads.

Fuels and feedstocks

When oil is combusted, an *exothermic** reaction occurs producing heat energy. Most crude oil (about 90%) is used as fuel. The remaining 10% is used as a raw material in the chemical industry and is known as **chemical feedstocks**. Refinery gas and naptha (a part of the gasoline fraction) are the main fractions found in chemical feedstocks.

Cracking

There is far more demand for the lighter fractions of oil, such as gasoline, than for the heavier fractions. To satisfy demand, the heavy fractions, with their larger molecules, are broken down into smaller molecules in a process called **cracking**. Cracking is carried out at very high temperatures. A *catalyst** is sometimes used.

*Exothermic, 32; Catalyst, 35.

Alkanes and alkenes

Organic molecules consist of carbon atoms each with four *covalent bonds**. These bonds enable carbon-based molecules to form long chains with other atoms. Organic molecules with the same atoms, bonded in the same way to carbon atoms, are grouped into families called **homologous series**. Alkanes, alkenes and alcohols are all examples of homologous series.

Within each series, the only difference in structure between each type of molecule is the number of carbon atoms present. Members of a homologous series share the same chemical

properties, but their physical properties change gradually as you descend the series.

Organic molecules are given names based on the homologous series they belong to and the number of carbon atoms they contain.

No. of carbon atoms	Homologous series		
	Alkane -ane	Alkene -ene	Alcohol -anol
1 Meth-	CH_4 Meth-ane		CH_3OH Meth-anol
2 Eth-	C_2H_6 Eth-ane	C_2H_4 Eth-ene	CH_3CH_2OH Eth-anol
3 Prop-	C_3H_8 Prop-ane	C_3H_6 Prop-ene	$CH_3CH_2CH_2OH$ Prop-anol

Alkanes

Alkanes are the simplest type of hydrocarbon. They all contain carbon atoms with each one bonded to four other atoms. For example, methane, has one carbon atom which forms bonds with four hydrogen atoms. Each alkane in the series has one more carbon atom, and two more hydrogen atoms, than the one before. Alkanes therefore have the *general formula** C_nH_{2n+2}.

An ethane molecule

Chemical formula C_2H_6

2 carbon atoms

n=2, therefore 2n+2=6

The first three alkane molecules

Name	Structural formulae*	Formula	A_r*	No. carbon atoms	Boiling point	Energy of combustion*
Methane	H H–C–H H	CH_4	16	1	-161°C	-890kJmol⁻¹
Ethane	H H H–C–C–H H H	C_2H_6	30	2	-89°C	-1560kJmol⁻¹
Propane	H H H H–C–C–C–H H H H	C_3H_8	44	3	-42°C	-2220kJmol⁻¹

Alkanes are called **saturated** molecules because no more atoms can be added to them. As a result, alkanes do not react easily with other atoms or molecules. They are insoluble in water, but dissolve in organic *solvents** such as benzene. Alkanes are very important fuels. They burn cleanly,

producing much energy.

Alkanes can undergo reactions in which one atom swaps places with another. This is called a **substitution reaction**. For example, one of methane's hydrogen atoms can swap places with a chlorine atom, creating chloromethane and hydrogen chloride.

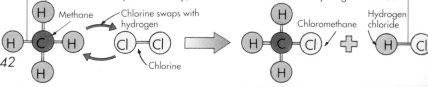

Methane — Chlorine swaps with hydrogen — Chlorine

Chloromethane — Hydrogen chloride

42

Alkenes

Alkenes, like alkanes, are made up of both carbon and hydrogen atoms. Their structures differ from alkanes in that they have a double bond between two of their carbon atoms. This double bond enables atoms to be added to alkenes during a chemical reaction. Alkenes are therefore called **unsaturated** molecules and are more reactive than alkanes. Alkenes can also be used as fuels by being burned in excess oxygen. They produce a smoky, yellow flame.

Ethene, an important alkene, is produced on a large scale by *cracking* the heavier fractions of crude oil. Ethene can also be prepared in the laboratory by passing *ethanol* vapour over a *dehydrating agent* such as aluminium oxide (Al_2O_3).

Laboratory preparation of ethene

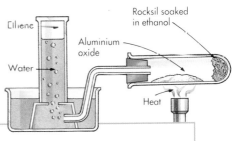

Reactions of alkenes

When alkenes react, the double bond between the two carbon atoms is broken. The atoms in the other *reagent* are added to the alkene. This is called an **addition reaction**. For example, in the diagram, the bromine molecules bond with ethene to form 1,2-dibromoethane, an important additive in petrol. This reaction results in bromine losing its brown colour. All alkenes decolourize both bromine and acidified potassium permanganate (which is a purple solution). This decolourizing can be used to distinguish between alkenes and alkanes.

Ethene   Bromine   1,2-dibromoethane

Hydrogenation and hydration

When hydrogen is heated with an alkene in the presence of a nickel *catalyst*, the hydrogen atoms in the hydrogen molecule combine with the alkene molecule to form an alkane. This is called **hydrogenation**.

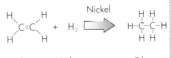

Ethene   Hydrogen   Ethane

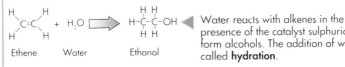

Ethene   Water   Ethanol

Water reacts with alkenes in the presence of the catalyst sulphuric acid to form alcohols. The addition of water is called **hydration**.

Isomers

Both alkanes and alkenes can form compounds called **isomers**, which have the same set of atoms, but are joined in different ways. They have the same chemical formula but different structural formulae. For example, butane (C_4H_{10}) has two isomers:

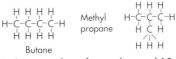

Both isomers have four carbon and 10 hydrogen atoms, but they are arranged in different ways.

*Covalent bonds, 13; General formula, 58; Solvents, 50; A_r, 7; Structural formulae, 3; Energy of Combustion, 58; Cracking, 41; Ethanol, 45; Dehydrating agent, 38; Reagent, 16.

Polymers

Polymers are organic compounds which contain enormously long chains of atoms. These chains are made up of small repeating units of molecules called **monomers**. Some polymers, such as starch, occur naturally. Others, such as nylon, are man-made and are called **synthetic polymers**. Chemists can make a vast range of synthetic polymers to serve particular purposes.

Plastics

Plastics are a large group of synthetic polymers which have had a tremendous impact on our everyday lives. All plastics have a number of useful qualities in common. They are strong as well as being light and flexible, easily coloured and moulded into shape. In addition, they are good heat insulators and are rot and corrosion-proof.

The alkene, ethene, forms the basis of many important plastics. For example, under the right conditions, ethene molecules will react with each other, opening up their double bonds and joining together to form the polymer **(poly)ethene**, or **polythene**. This process is known as **addition polymerization**.

Addition polymerization

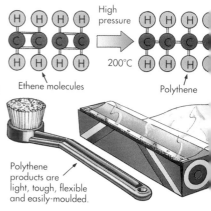

Ethene molecules → Polythene

Polythene products are light, tough, flexible and easily-moulded.

Thermosoftening and thermosetting plastics

Plastics which soften and melt when heated, but do not change their structure, are called **thermosoftening** plastics. They are flexible and can be remoulded and used again, but are not very heat resistant. PVC, nylon, polystyrene and polythene are all thermosoftening plastics.

Plastics which can be heated, melted and moulded once only are called **thermosetting** plastics. Their molecules are fixed rigidly in place which makes them hard and heat-resistant. Bakelite is a thermosetting plastic. It was one of the first plastics invented and is still used for light fittings. Melamine is also a thermosetting plastic. It is used for kitchen worktops.

Problems with plastics

Plastics in rubbish can give off methane gas which can be explosive.

Rainwater seeps through the rubbish forming a toxic slime called **leachate**. Leachate is harmful if it leaks into underground water supplies.

Most plastics are made from raw materials derived from crude oil. They are difficult to recycle, so many of the resources used to create them cannot be reclaimed. Most plastics cannot be burned as they release toxic fumes. They do not decay naturally and so are called **non-biodegradable**.

Most non-biodegradable rubbish is buried in huge holes dug deep into the ground. These are called **landfill sites**. In addition to the large amount of land they take up, landfill sites have a number of serious drawbacks.

Water supply

Alcohols

Alcohols form a *homologous series**. The first four in the series are:

Name	Formula	Structural formulae*
Methanol	CH_3OH	H H–C–OH H
Ethanol	C_2H_5OH	H H H–C–C–OH H H
Propan-1-ol	C_3H_7OH	H H H H–C–C–C–H H H OH
Propan-2-ol	C_3H_7OH	H H H H–C–C–C–H H OH H

Propan-1-ol and propan-2-ol are *isomers**.

Ethanol

Alcohols are an important group of organic compounds. They are different from *alkanes** and *alkenes** in that their structure does not consist exclusively of carbon and hydrogen atoms. Ethanol is the most important of the alcohols. It is a clear, sweet-smelling, water-soluble liquid which evaporates quickly.

Ethanol is widely used in industry as a *solvent** for many substances, including paints, dyes and perfumes. It burns with a clean blue flame, produces a lot of heat and doesn't give off pollutants such as sulphur and nitrous oxides. It is occasionally used as a fuel in some countries and may become more important in the future.

Alcoholic fermentation

Ethanol is the potent substance found in alcoholic drinks. Alcohol in drinks can give people pleasure, but it can cause serious damage when consumed in excess.

Ethanol can be made by adding yeast to a sugar, in a process called **alcoholic fermentation**. This process has been used for thousands of years to make beer and wine. The equation for fermentation using glucose as the sugar is shown below.

$$C_6H_{12}O_6 \longrightarrow 2C_2H_5OH + 2CO_2$$

Glucose — Yeast → Ethanol + Carbon dioxide

Substances in yeast, called **enzymes**, act as *catalysts** in the process during which sugar is broken down into ethanol. After a time the ethanol produced during fermentation will kill the yeast. To obtain pure ethanol, the mixture left is separated by *fractional distillation**.

Laboratory fermentation

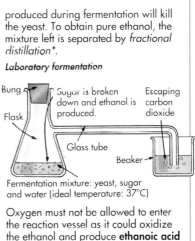

Oxygen must not be allowed to enter the reaction vessel as it could oxidize the ethanol and produce **ethanoic acid** (CH_3COOH). Vinegar is a weak solution of ethanoic acid.

Industrial production of ethanol

Most of the ethanol used in industry is made, not by alcoholic fermentation, but by an *addition reaction** between ethene and steam. This is shown below.

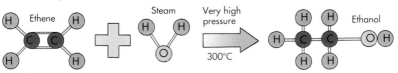

*Homologous series, 42; Structural formulae, 3; Isomers, 43; Alkanes, 42; Alkenes, 43; Solvent, 50; Catalysts, 35; Fractional distillation, 51; Addition reaction, 43.

The problems of the chemical industry

The chemical industry has provided people with enormous benefits, from increased food production to new drugs to fight diseases. It employs many people and is a major factor in the growth of modern industry. However, in addition to the benefits, there are problems. Many of these are related to aspects of pollution which have been discussed earlier in this book (see air pollution, pages 10-11, water pollution, page 30-31, and landfill sites, page 44).

Siting industrial plants

Many factors, apart from pollution, influence the siting of a chemical plant. These can be split into two groups: technical and financial issues, and social and ecological factors.

The issues considered by the organization responsible for building and running the plant tend to be technical and financial ones. Examples of such considerations are the need for raw materials, land, transport links and a suitable workforce nearby. All these factors need to be available at an affordable price, making the site as profitable as possible.

The social and environmental factors are ones which affect the local community and its surroundings. These give rise to questions concerning potential waste, pollution and noise generated by the plant, as well as safety risks associated with the particular substance manufactured. There is also the question of whether the plant will overburden the community, or benefit the area by bringing money and employment.

Both types of factor have been considered in the example below.

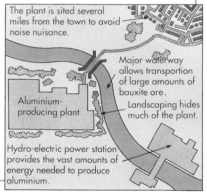

The plant is sited several miles from the town to avoid noise nuisance.

Major waterway allows transportation of large amounts of bauxite ore.

Landscaping hides much of the plant.

Aluminium-producing plant

Hydro-electric power station provides the vast amounts of energy needed to produce aluminium.

Acid rain

When *fossil fuels** containing sulphur are burned, they produce sulphur dioxide. Nitrogen in the air is normally unreactive but it reacts at high temperatures (such as inside a car engine) to form nitrogen oxides. Sulphur dioxide and nitrogen oxides are toxic acidic gases which can cause chest and lung diseases. They react with rain water to form sulphurous, nitric and nitrous acids which give rain a far greater acidity than normal. This is known as **acid rain**.

Acid rain *corrodes** metals and the stonework of buildings. It also frees some metal *ions** which were previously 'locked' safely in soil particles. These can cause harm by, for example, changing the *pH** of water in rivers and lakes. This, in turn, kills aquatic life.

The level of acid rain can be reduced by burning fewer fossil fuels, removing sulphur and nitrogen from fuels, and refining engines to cut down harmful emissions.

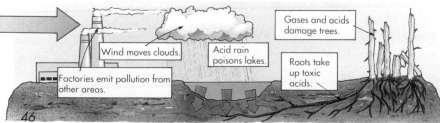

Gases and acids damage trees.

Wind moves clouds.

Acid rain poisons lakes.

Roots take up toxic acids.

Factories emit pollution from other areas.

*Fossil fuels, 40; Corrode, 24; Ions, 12; pH, 25.

Ozone depletion

Dangerous ultra-violet rays from the sun can cause skin cancer. The earth is protected from these rays by a layer of ozone (O_3) molecules found in the atmosphere. However, substances called **chlorofluorocarbons** (CFCs), used in aerosols, fridges and the manufacture of polystyrene, are attacking and destroying this layer. International action has been taken to reduce CFC emissions, but many scientists would like to see more done.

A Total Ozone Map

There is a shortage of ozone over the Antarctic. This was discovered in 1985.

Purple indicates lowest amount of ozone.

The greenhouse effect

Carbon dioxide plays an important role in warming the earth by trapping the sun's heat. This is called the **greenhouse effect**. For millions of years the *carbon cycle** maintained a balance between the processes that add and those that take away carbon dioxide from the air.

In modern times, people have upset this balance by burning vast amounts of fossil fuels, and so releasing excess carbon dioxide into the atmosphere. A lot of tropical rainforest has been destroyed, which in turn has reduced the amount of carbon dioxide used up by green plants during *photosynthesis**. This has resulted in an increase in carbon dioxide (CO_2) in the air.

As the concentration of carbon dioxide in the air increases, more heat energy is trapped. Less can escape out of the atmosphere and the average temperature of the earth's surface gradually increases. It is believed that other gases, such as methane and the ozone-destroying CFC's, act in a similar way to carbon dioxide. Scientists are in doubt as to precisely how much temperatures will rise as a result of the continued emission of these gases. However, they argue that it could possibly cause severe changes in climate.

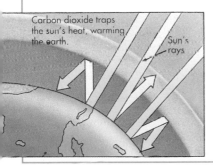

Carbon dioxide traps the sun's heat, warming the earth.

Sun's rays

Chemicals in the home and laboratory

Some household chemicals, such as bleach and glue, are dangerous if inhaled or drunk. They should always be kept out of the reach of small children.

Substances in the laboratory can be dangerous in a number of ways. They can, for example, be *radioactive**, harmful if inhaled, or corrosive to the skin and worksurfaces. To handle chemicals with care, you need to know in what way they may be hazardous. Chemical hazard symbols (see below) act as warnings telling you what to beware of. They are found as labels on containers of substances and at entrances to dangerous areas.

| Toxic | Toxic (USA) | Harmful | Flammable | Oxidizing | Explosive |

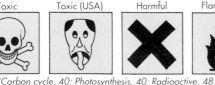

*Carbon cycle, 40; Photosynthesis, 40; Radioactive, 48.

Nuclear power and radiation

In a chemical reaction it is only the number of electrons in the outer shell that change. A **nuclear reaction** is one which involves changes to the nucleus itself. The nuclei of some types of atom are unstable, which causes them to break up. When they do, they emit waves and particles called **radiation**, in a process called **radioactive decay**. There are three types of radiation: **alpha particles** (helium nuclei), **beta particles** (streams of electrons) and **gamma rays** (high energy *waves**). They can be identified by the distance they can travel.

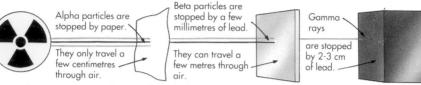

Alpha particles are stopped by paper.

They only travel a few centimetres through air.

Beta particles are stopped by a few millimetres of lead.

They can travel a few metres through air.

Gamma rays are stopped by 2-3 cm of lead.

Scientists measure the speed at which radioactive decay occurs (known as the **rate of decay**) in half-lives. A **half-life** is the time it takes for half of a radioactive substance (known as a **radioisotope**) to disintegrate. This rate varies from substance to substance. For example, carbon-14 has a half life of 5500 years, whereas radium-221's half life measures just 30 seconds. The longer the half life, the slower the rate of decay and the more stable the radioisotope.

Uses and problems of radiation

Radioactive materials are used to treat certain types of cancer. Some radioisotopes, such as cobalt-60, are used to detect flaws in metals and to measure the thickness of paper and plastics.

Carbon-14 is a radioisotope found in all living things. It starts to decay after the organism dies. As carbon-14's half-life is known, the age of a sample can be calculated by measuring how much carbon-14 is left in it. This process is called **radiocarbon dating**.

Although radiation can be of use, it is extremely dangerous and is lethal in large doses. It can destroy or damage living tissue and can cause skin burns, sickness, sterility and various forms of cancer. Scientists, doctors and energy personnel who work with radioactive materials must take many safety precautions. These include working behind lead shields and wearing protective clothing.

Archeologists use carbon-dating to establish the age of ancient artefacts.

Radiation hazard sign (see page 47).

Special badge indicates level of radiation encountered.

Nuclear power

Nuclear power produces cheap electricity without the pollution problems associated with burning fossil fuels. However, it does have a number of serious problems. Leaks from faulty power stations (such as Chernobyl in 1986) have resulted in many deaths both directly and through cancers. Many people worry about the likelihood of a nuclear power station explosion, which would result in massive devastation.

The safe disposal of nuclear waste is also a major concern. Some waste materials remain radioactive for many hundreds of years and must be sealed in containers that will not be disturbed. These containers are often buried deep underground or dropped onto the sea-bed.

48 *Waves, 59; Fossil fuels, 40.

The reactivity series

| Metal | Reaction with air | Reaction with water | | Reaction with dilute acids | Reaction of metal's oxides | | Solubility* | Reaction of heat and hydroxides* |
		Cold	Steam		With hydrogen	With carbon		
Potassium	Burn readily to form oxide	Explosive H_2 evolved*	Explosive H_2 evolved	Explosive H_2 evolved	No reaction	No reaction	Very soluble	No reaction
Sodium	Burn readily to form oxide	Violent H_2 evolved	Violent H_2 evolved	Violent H_2 evolved	No reaction	No reaction	Very soluble	No reaction
Calcium	Burn readily to form oxide	Quiet H_2 evolved	Strong H_2 evolved	Strong H_2 evolved	No reaction	No reaction	Slightly soluble	Decomposed* by heat to form oxide
Magnesium	Form oxide when heated	No reaction	Quiet H_2 evolved	Normal H_2 evolved	No reaction	No reaction	Sparingly soluble	Decomposed* by heat to form oxide
Aluminium	Form oxide when heated	No reaction	Reversible reaction	Normal H_2 evolved	No reaction	No reaction	Insoluble	Decomposed* by heat to form oxide
Zinc	Form oxide when heated	No reaction	Reversible reaction	Normal H_2 evolved	Reversible reaction	Reduced to metal Carbon dioxide formed	Insoluble	Decomposed* by heat to form oxide
Iron	Form oxide when heated	No reaction	Reversible reaction	Weak H_2 evolved	Reversible reaction	Reduced to metal Carbon dioxide formed	Insoluble	Decomposed* by heat to form oxide
Tin	Form oxide when heated	No reaction	No reaction	Weak H_2 evolved	Reduced* to metal Water formed	Reduced to metal Carbon dioxide formed	Insoluble	Decomposed* by heat to form oxide
Lead	No reaction	No reaction	No reaction	Weak H_2 evolved	Reduced* to metal Water formed	Reduced to metal Carbon dioxide formed	Insoluble	Decomposed* by heat to form oxide
Copper	Reversible reaction	No reaction	No reaction	No reaction	Oxides reduced to metal by heat only		Insoluble	Unstable or not formed
Mercury	Reversible reaction	No reaction	No reaction	No reaction	Oxides reduced to metal by heat only		Insoluble	Unstable or not formed
Silver	No reaction	No reaction	No reaction	No reaction	Oxides reduced to metal by heat only	Oxides reduced to metal by heat only	Insoluble	Unstable or not formed
Gold	No reaction	No reaction	No reaction	No reaction	Oxides reduced to metal by heat only	Oxides reduced to metal by heat only	Insoluble	Unstable or not formed

*Evolved, 58; Oxides, 59; Reduced, 18; Solubility, 50; Hydroxide, 58; Decomposed, 50.

Solubilities and separation

A solid that dissolves in a liquid is called a **solute** and is said to be **soluble**. The liquid that dissolves the solid is called a **solvent** and the resulting mixture is called a **solution**. For example, sodium chloride is soluble. It dissolves readily in water forming a colourless solution. Sand, on the other hand, is insoluble; it does not dissolve in water at all.

Most insoluble solids settle to the bottom of a liquid, but some split into tiny particles which spread throughout the liquid. This type of mixture is called a **suspension**. For example, milk is a suspension of fat particles in water.

The mass of a substance that dissolves in 100g of solvent is described as the **solubility** of that substance. Solubility can vary with temperature; plotted against temperature, it produces a **solubility curve**. When no more of a substance can be dissolved, the solution is said to be **saturated**.

Methods of separation

There are a number of methods of separating substances from each other. Some of the most commonly used techniques are shown below.

Simple distillation is similar to evaporation (see below), except that the evaporated liquid is collected after cooling. It is used for liquids with greatly differing boiling points and for obtaining pure solvent from a solution containing a dissolved solid.

A **Liebig condenser** speeds up the cooling and condensing process. The vapour passes through the condenser's centre and is cooled by water flowing round the condenser's outer wall.

Separating funnel
When two liquids completely mix with each other, such as water and ethanol, they are said to be **miscible**. Liquids which do not mix, such as oil and water, are **immiscible**. Two immiscible liquids can be split using a **separating funnel**.

A separating funnel

Two immiscible liquids

Tap

In the laboratory, *evaporation** is used to separate a solid dissolved in a liquid. The solution is boiled, which releases the liquid as a gas. This leaves the solid in the evaporating dish.

Evaporating basin

Solvent evaporates

Heat

Simple distillation

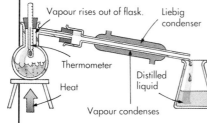

Vapour rises out of flask.

Liebig condenser

Thermometer

Distilled liquid

Heat

Vapour condenses

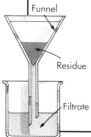

Funnel

Residue

Filtrate

Filtration is a method of separating a solid from a liquid, or an insoluble substance from a soluble one. The mixture is poured through a filter; the liquid that goes through is called the **filtrate**, the solid that remains behind is called the **residue**.

Centrifuging is a method in which a suspension is spun very quickly in a machine called a **centrifuge**. This forces the solid particles to the bottom of the container. The liquid can then be poured off. This method is used in hospitals to separate the red cells from the blood.

A laboratory centrifuge

*Evaporation, 58.

Fractional distillation

Fractional distillation is similar to simple distillation but uses an additional piece of apparatus called a **fractionating column**. A fractionating column contains glass rings or balls which provide a large surface area for condensation and re-evaporation. The vapour of the liquid with the lowest boiling point reaches the top of the column first. Fractional distillation is used to separate liquids with close boiling points.

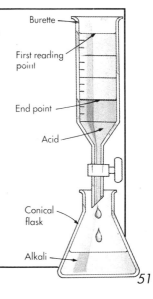

Thermometer

Glass beads

Liebeg condenser

Fractionating column

Heat

Chromatography

Chromatography is the method used to separate several substances dissolved in a solvent. A spot of the mixture to be separated is placed near the bottom of some filter paper and solvent added. The different components in the solution move up the paper with the solvent, but

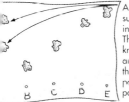

A, an unknown substance, breaks up into two substances. These must be the known substances, C and D because of their matching positions on the filter paper.

B C D E

at different speeds. Eventually, the substances are separated out and remain as distinct spots or bands on the paper. This is called a **chromatogram**.

Chromatography is only suitable for separating very small quantities. It is mainly used as a purity test, but also to determine what a substance consists of.

A chromatogram can be made of some known pure substances and one unknown. The positions of the different components of the unknown substance are compared to those of the known substances. This method is used, for example, to determine the different dyes in ink.

Titration

The **concentration** of a solution is the number of *moles** of a substance dissolved in $1dm^3$ of solvent. Finding the concentration of a solution is called **volumetric analysis**. Two solutions, one of known and one of unknown concentration, are mixed together using a measuring vessel called a **burette**. This technique is known as a **titration**.

A measure of one solution is placed in the burette. It is gradually added to the second solution until the two solutions have finished their reaction. The solution remaining in the burette is measured. This is called the **end point**. The original amount in the burette, minus the end point, gives you the amount of solution used. From this, calculations can be made to assess the concentration of the unknown solution.

The most common type of titration is an **acid-base titration**. An acid solution of known concentration is added to a base solution of unknown concentration. An *indicator** is used to find the end point.

Burette

First reading point

End point

Acid

Conical flask

Alkali

*Moles, 28; Indicator, 26.

Practical experiments

Analysis of salts

The *cation** present in a salt can usually be identified by a **flame test**. A tiny sample of the unknown salt is added to concentrated hydrochloric acid. This is placed on the end of a clean piece of platinum wire and ignited in a bunsen flame. Different cations produce different colours in the bunsen flame.

A bright yellow colour — sodium
A lilac colour — potassium
A brick-red colour — calcium
A blue-green colour — copper

The ammonium cation (NH_4^+) does not have a distinctive flame colour, but can be detected because it gives off ammonia gas when sodium hydroxide is added to it. Ammonia has a pungent smell and turns damp red litmus paper blue.

There are a number of tests for the different types of *anion** found in a salt. Carbonates, which contain the CO_3^{2-} ion, give off carbon dioxide when an acid is added. Sulphates, which contain the SO_4^{2-} ion, produce a white *precipitate** when barium chloride and hydrochloric acid are added. Chlorides, which contain the Cl^- ion, produce a white precipitate when silver nitrate and dilute nitric acid are added.

Salts that react with both acids and bases are called **amphoteric salts**. If an excess of sodium hydroxide is added, for example, to zinc hydroxide it will react and the precipitate will dissolve.

Testing for purity

Pure substances all have fixed melting and boiling points at a set *pressure**. An impure solid has a lower melting point than a pure solid. An impure liquid has a higher boiling point than a pure one.

For example, 10 cm³ of pure water has 1g measures of salt added to it at regular intervals. In between each extra addition, the solution is heated and its boiling point taken. A graph can then be plotted. This shows that the more salt in the water, the higher the solution's boiling point.

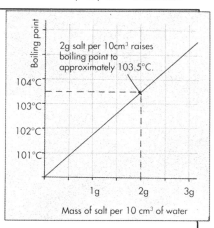

2g salt per 10cm³ raises boiling point to approximately 103.5°C.

Mass of salt per 10 cm³ of water

Measuring a melting point

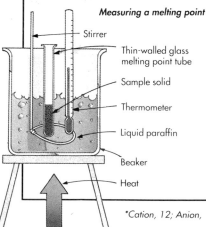

- Stirrer
- Thin-walled glass melting point tube
- Sample solid
- Thermometer
- Liquid paraffin
- Beaker
- Heat

Measuring a melting point requires more *apparatus** than measuring a typical boiling point. A sample of the substance is placed in a thin walled glass tube. The tube and a thermometer are then suspended in a bath of liquid paraffin. The bath is slowly heated and an even temperature is maintained by constant stirring. When the sample melts (turns from solid to liquid), the temperature can be recorded. This temperature can be compared against the melting point of the pure substance.

*Cation, 12; Anion, 12; Precipitate, 59; Pressure, 5; Apparatus, 60.

Gases in the laboratory

Preparation of nitrogen

Impure nitrogen is produced by removing oxygen and carbon dioxide from air. This leaves nitrogen with some residue of water vapour and *noble gases**. The oxygen is removed by passing the air over heated copper. The carbon dioxide is removed by passing air through sodium hydroxide solution.

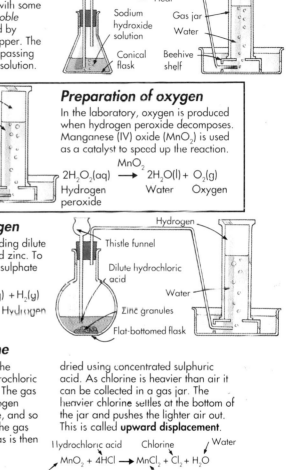

Preparation of oxygen

In the laboratory, oxygen is produced when hydrogen peroxide decomposes. Manganese (IV) oxide (MnO_2) is used as a catalyst to speed up the reaction.

$$2H_2O_2(aq) \xrightarrow{MnO_2} 2H_2O(l) + O_2(g)$$

Hydrogen peroxide   Water   Oxygen

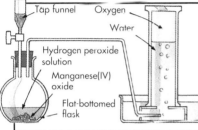

Preparation of hydrogen

Hydrogen can be made by adding dilute hydrochloric acid to granulated zinc. To speed up the reaction, copper sulphate solution can be added.

$$Zn(s) + 2HCl(aq) \longrightarrow ZnCl_2(aq) + H_2(g)$$

Zinc   Hydrochloric acid   Zinc chloride   Hydrogen

Preparation of chlorine

Chlorine is prepared through the oxidation of concentrated hydrochloric acid by manganese(IV) oxide. The gas produced contains some hydrogen chloride which is water soluble, and so can be removed by bubbling the gas through water. The chlorine gas is then dried using concentrated sulphuric acid. As chlorine is heavier than air it can be collected in a gas jar. The heavier chlorine settles at the bottom of the jar and pushes the lighter air out. This is called **upward displacement**.

$$MnO_2 + 4HCl \longrightarrow MnCl_2 + Cl_2 + H_2O$$

Hydrochloric acid   Chlorine   Water
Manganese(IV) oxide   Manganese(IV) chloride

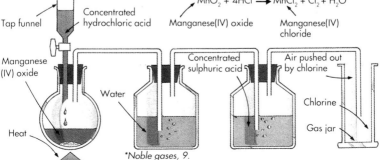

*Noble gases, 9.

Percentage of oxygen in the air

The amount of oxygen in the air can be found by using the *apparatus** below. A specified amount of air is passed from the left hand gas syringe over heated copper in a glass tube. The heated copper combines with the oxygen in the air to form black copper oxide. The remaining elements of air enter the previously empty right hand gas syringe.

The air is repeatedly passed from the left to the right syringe over the heated copper and back again. This continues until all of the oxygen has reacted with the copper. (This is when there is no further change in the volumes of air found in the gas syringes.) The apparatus is left to cool and then a reading of the volume of air (minus the oxygen) is taken from one of the syringes. The percentage of oxygen in air is calculated using the following formula:

$$\frac{\% \text{ oxygen}}{\text{in air}} = \frac{\text{decrease in volume of air}}{\text{initial volume of air}}$$

In the example below, 200 cm^3 of air is used in the apparatus. The decrease in the volume of air is 42 cm^3. Using the calculation above, the precentage of oxygen in air is found to be 21%.

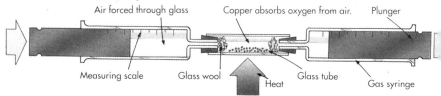

Air forced through glass — Copper absorbs oxygen from air. — Plunger

Measuring scale — Glass wool — Heat — Glass tube — Gas syringe

Identifying gases

Measuring the amount of a substance in a reaction is called **quantitative analysis**. Identifying a particular substance in a reaction is called **qualitative analysis**. Tests to identify gases are forms of qualitative analysis. Testing for carbon dioxide is described on page 21, and for oxygen on page 10.

The table below shows the methods used to identify a number of other gases.

Name	Formula	Colour	Test
Ammonia	NH_3	Colourless	Red litmus paper is turned blue.
Bromine	Br_2	Red/brown	Forms a yellow solution in water.
Hydrogen	H_2	Colourless	Burns with a pop forming water.
Nitrogen monoxide	NO	Colourless	Forms brown fumes when in air.
Sulphur dioxide	SO_2	Colourless	Turns potassium dichromate (VI) orange to green.
Chlorine	Cl_2	Pale green	Blue litmus paper is turned red.
Ethene	C_2H_4	Colourless	Takes bromine's colour away. Burns to form carbon dioxide and water.
Methane	CH_2	Colourless	Burns with a blue flame, forming carbon dioxide and water.
Nitrogen	N_2	Colourless	Puts out a burning splint and does not react with lime water.
Nitrogen dioxide	NO_2	Brown	Forms an acidic and colourless solution when mixed with water.

Table of Elements

Below is table of the elements you are most likely to deal with when learning about chemistry. They are listed along with some of their key properties.

Element	Symbol	Atomic No.*	A$_r$*	Valency*	Boiling point (°C)	Melting point (°C)
Aluminium	Al	13	27	3	2470	660
Argon	Ar	18	40	1	-186	-189
Barium	Ba	56	137	2	1640	714
Beryllium	Be	4	9	1, 2	2477	1280
Boron	B	5	11	1, 3	3930	2300
Bromine	Br	35	80	1, 5, 7	58.8	-7.2
Calcium	Ca	20	40	2	1487	850
Carbon (diamond)	C	6	12	4	Unknown	3750
Carbon (graphite)	C	6	12	4	4830	3730†
Chlorine	Cl	17	35.5	1, 7, 5	-34.7	-101
Chromium	Cr	24	52	3, 6	2482	1890
Copper	Cu	29	64	1, 2	2595	1083
Fluorine	F	9	19	1, 7	-188	-220
Gold	Au	79	197	1, 2, 3	2970	1063
Helium	He	2	4	1	-269	-270
Hydrogen	H	1	1	1	-252	-259
Iodine	I	53	127	1, 5, 7	184	114
Iron	Fe	26	56	2, 3	3000	1535
Lead	Pb	82	207	2, 4	1744	327
Lithium	Li	3	7	1	1330	180
Magnesium	Mg	12	24	2	1110	650
Manganese	Mn	25	55	2, 3, 4, 7	2100	1240
Mercury	Hg	80	201	1, 2	357	-38.9
Neon	Ne	10	20	1	-246	-249
Nickel	Ni	28	59	2	2730	1453
Nitrogen	N	7	14	3, 5	-196	-210
Oxygen	O	8	16	2	-183	-218
Phosphorus (white)	P	15	31	3, 5	280	44.2
Platinum	Pt	78	195	2, 4	4530	1769
Plutonium	Pu	94	242	3, 4, 5, 6	3240	640
Potassium	K	19	39	1	774	63.7
Silicon	Si	14	28	4	2360	1410
Silver	Ag	47	108	1	2210	961
Sodium	Na	11	23	1	890	97.8
Sulphur (monoclinic)	S	16	32	2, 4, 6	444	119
Tin	Sn	50	119	2, 4	1730	1540
Titanium	Ti	22	48	1, 2, 3, 4	3260	1675
Tungsten	W	74	184	4, 6	5930	3410
Uranium	U	92	238	3, 4, 5, 6	3820	1130
Xenon	Xe	54	131	1	-108	-112
Zinc	Zn	30	65	2	907	420

†Graphite *sublimes** at this temperature.

Chemistry who's who

The list below contains short biographies of a number of the most influential chemists.

Much of modern chemistry has developed from skills such as metalworking and simple recipes for medicines, dyes and other everyday things. Chemistry gets its name from the Arabic word, *al quemia* meaning alchemy. Alchemy was an early form of chemistry practised in the Middle East from Roman times, and later in Europe.

Among other things, alchemists believed they could make gold out of more common metals. Much of their work was surrounded by magic and superstition, but alchemists did make many useful discoveries and evolved techniques which paved the way for modern chemistry. Modern chemical practice is generally considered to date from the 17th century with the work of scientists such as Robert Boyle.

Amedeo Avogadro (1776-1856) Italian. Trained as a lawyer then turned to physics and chemistry in his thirties. He was the first to point out that equal volumes of gas at the same temperature and pressure contain the same number of particles. This led to the realization that one mole of any substance contains the same number of particles, the *Avogadro number**.

Antoine Becquerel (1852-1908) French. Came from a distinguished family of scientists and succeeded his father as professor of physics at a college in Paris in 1895. A year later, he found that a uranium salt placed on a wrapped photographic plate gave out invisible rays which made the plate blacken: these rays were *radiation**. In 1903 he shared a Nobel Prize with Marie and Pierre Curie (see below).

Neils Bohr (1885-1962) Danish. Born in Copenhagen, he created the first modern theory of how the atom is constructed. He worked in England for a time before becoming Director of the Institute of Theoretical Physics in Copenhagen. In 1922, he won the Nobel Prize. Escaping Nazi Europe in 1943, he moved to England and worked on the Atomic bomb programme. He was actively anti-nuclear in later years.

Robert Boyle (1627-91) Irish.
Came from the Irish aristocracy and is best known for his work with pressures and volumes of gases. His important Boyle's Law is illustrated opposite. His book, 'The Sceptical Chymist' rejected old ideas and insisted on scientific methods of experiment and observation. He also proposed the notion of simple elements which could be combined to form compounds.

Wallace Carothers (1896-1937) American. He was the first chemist to make a synthetic fibre. He worked for a company called Du Pont and synthesized the synthetic rubber, Neoprene, marketed in 1932. He went on to produce nylon which had huge commercial success and is still widely used today. Carothers is considered the father of the plastics industry. He suffered from depression and committed suicide at the age of 41.

Henry Cavendish (1731-1810) British. An eccentric recluse, Cavendish inherited a vast fortune which he used to finance his experiments. He devoted his life to science and was one of the first chemists to study gas reactions. One of his most important discoveries was that water was a compound and not an element.

Marie Curie (1867-1934) French. Discovered the radioactive element radium and conducted pioneering work (with her husband Pierre) into radioactivity. She was considered to be a chemist and physicist of world standing despite living and working in a male-dominated world. She won Nobel Prizes, twice, once in 1903 and again in 1911. She died in 1934 from leukaemia caused by exposure to radioactive materials.

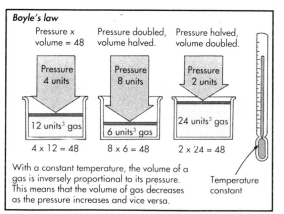

Boyle's law

Pressure x volume = 48 — Pressure 4 units — 12 units³ gas — 4 × 12 = 48

Pressure doubled, volume halved. — Pressure 8 units — 6 units³ gas — 8 × 6 = 48

Pressure halved, volume doubled. — Pressure 2 units — 24 units³ gas — 2 × 24 = 48

Temperature constant

With a constant temperature, the volume of a gas is inversely proportional to its pressure. This means that the volume of gas decreases as the pressure increases and vice versa.

*Avogadro number, 28; Radiation, 48; Boyle's Law, 58.

John Dalton (1766-1844) British.
The son of a Quaker, Dalton spent most of his life in an isolated village in Cumbria working as a school teacher. Famous for his innovations on the subject of atomic theory, he was the first to suggest that molecules are made from atoms combined in simple ratios.

Michael Faraday (1791-1867) British.
Faraday was both a physicist and chemist. He discovered the compound benzene in 1825 and was the founder of the area of chemistry known as *electrochemistry**. It was through his discoveries that the modern battery was developed. He contributed greatly to the understanding of electricity and the electronic properties of certain solutions. He was a deeply religious man who despite gaining fame, lived in a simple, modest way.

Joseph Gay-Lussac (1778-1850) French.
Although he is most well-known for his experiments with gases, Gay-Lussac was also the first to use chemistry to prepare sodium and potassium, as well as isolating boron. A pioneering hot air balloonist, Gay-Lussac held the world altitude record of approximately 7500 metres for many years.

Fritz Haber (1868-1934) German.
The inventor of the *Haber Process** to manufacture ammonia on an industrial scale. His work is said to have prolonged the First World War by two years, as it enabled Germany to manufacture explosives long after natural supplies of ammonia-yielding compounds had been exhausted.
  He was of Jewish ancestry and, although a fervent patriot, was hated by the Nazis. He fled to England in the early 1930's.

Dorothy Hodgkin (1910-) British.
The first chemist to use X-rays to find the exact structure of complex molecules. Hodgkin's successes include the mapping of penicillin, vitamin B_{12} and insulin. Her work has had important applications for the pharmaceutical industry. She won the Nobel Prize for Chemistry in 1964.

Antoine Lavoisier (1743-1794) French.
Lavoisier was the first to apply the principle of conservation of mass to writing chemical equations. He also introduced principles for naming substances that are still in use today.
  Lavoisier experimented with gases, demonstrating the properties of oxygen and showing that water is made up of oxygen and hydrogen. He criticised the scientific ideas of Marat, one of the leaders of the French Revolution, and was guillotined in 1794.

Dmitrii Mendeleev (1834-1907) Russian.
Mendeleev was one of 14 children and grew up in Siberia. At the age of 15 his mother took him to St Petersburg where he became a highly successful student, and later a researcher and lecturer at the University. He created the periodic table of elements in 1869.

Alfred Nobel (1833-1896) Swedish.
The son of an inventor. In 1842, Nobel's family moved to Russia where he gained a scientific education. He finally settled in Sweden in 1859, after living in Paris and Russia. Nobel invented dynamite in a highly dangerous process that severely maimed him, killed his brother and, in one explosion, took five lives. He died extremely rich and bestowed money to create the annual Nobel Prizes.

Linus Pauling (1901-) American.
Creator of the modern *covalent** theory of bonding. Pauling also showed that sickle cell disease could be traced to changes occuring in the structure of important molecules in a victim's blood. He has won two Nobel Prizes, one for chemistry in 1954 and the Peace Prize in 1962. He is a controversial but highly respected figure in the world of science, and undoubtedly one of the greatest chemists of the 20th Century.

Joseph Priestley (1733-1804) British.
Although he had no formal scientific training, Priestley constructed numerous experiments. In 1774, he discovered oxygen and eventually identified most of the common gases.
  Priestley was a schoolteacher, writer and politician, whose radical views on the French Revolution were so unpopular that he emigrated to the United States.

Ernest Rutherford (1871-1937)
New Zealander.
Originally interested in the phenomenon that became known as radio waves, Rutherford worked with J.J. Thomson at Cambridge, succeeding him as Professor there. Rutherford detailed the structure of the atom and was the first person to split an atom. For his work in determining the different types of radiation particles, Rutherford won a Nobel Prize in 1908.

J.J. Thomson (1851-1940) British.
Became a Professor at Cambridge at the age of only 28. His pioneering experimental work led to the discovery of the electron. He also discovered that gases could be made to conduct electricity, so paving the way for radio, television and radar. For this latter research, Thomson was awarded a Nobel Prize in 1906.

*Electrochemistry, 58; Haber process, 36; Covalent, 13.

Glossary

This glossary defines some of the more common terms used in chemistry which are not fully defined in the main text. Any word in the text of an entry which has its own entry in the glossary is followed by a † sign.

Abrasive. A substance capable of rubbing or grinding down another substance. Sand can be described as an abrasive.

Abundance. The measure of how much of a substance exists. It is often expressed as percentage. For example, silicon is the second most abundant element on earth.

Allotrope. An element that exists in more than one form. For example, diamond and graphite are both solid allotropes of the element carbon. Sulphur has five different allotropes.

Aqueous solution. A solution which has water as its *solvent**. For example, an aqueous solution of ammonia is produced by dissolving ammonia gas in water. An aqueous solution found in an equation is denoted by the state symbol (aq).

Bleach. A substance used to remove colour from a material or solution. Sunlight and oxygen act as bleaches. The most commonly used bleach is sodium chlorate (NaClO). It is formed when sodium hydroxide solution is reacted with chlorine. Household bleaches and cleaners frequently contain sodium chlorate.

Carbon-12. One of the three *isotopes** of the element, carbon, carbon-12 is used as a reference for the calculation of both *relative atomic mass** and the *mole**.

Crystal. A solid whose atoms are arranged in a definite geometric pattern. The edges of crystals are straight and the surfaces flat.

Decompose. To break down substances into other substances. For example, heat decomposes lead(II) nitrate into lead(II) oxide, nitrogen dioxide and oxygen, as shown in the equation below:

$$2Pb(NO_3)_2(s) \longrightarrow 2PbO(s) + 4NO_2(g) + O_2(g)$$

Density. The mass† of a substance divided by its volume† and stated in units of g/cm^3. A substance with a large mass occupying a small volume (such as lead) has a high density. Many gases, have a low mass occupying a large volume. They have a low density. Every substance has its own different density. This helps in identifying substances.

Effervescence. The escape of bubbles of gas from a liquid. A glass of lemonade is described as being effervescent.

Elastic. A solid which can have its shape changed by force, but which returns to its original shape when the force disappears or is removed. For example, rubber is elastic.

Electrochemistry. The branch of chemistry which deals with electrolysis and electricity related areas.

Energy of combustion. The amount of energy released when one mole of a substance burns completely. For example, the energy of combustion of methane is 890 kilojoules per mole.

Evaporation. The change in state of a substance from a liquid to a gas or vapour, at a temperature below the liquid's boiling point. Evaporation requires heat energy and occurs from the surface of the liquid.

Evolve. To form bubbles of a gas during a reaction and then to give off that gas. For example, carbon dioxide is evolved when methane is combusted.

Flammable. A substance which will burst into flames under the right conditions. Inflammable is another word for flammable. Non-flammable is the opposite of flammable.

Food web. A diagram to show how animals obtain energy from different sources. For example, a stickleback in a small pond may eat watersnails and tadpoles which themselves feed on pondweed and algae. A break in the web (for example, a wiping out of algae due to chemical pollution) can be disasterous to the whole web.

Geiger-Muller tube. Commonly known as a geiger counter, it is an instrument used to measure *radioactivity**. When a radioactive particle or ray enters the tube, an argon atom *ionizes**, releasing an electron. The electrons discharge and register as a series of clicks or meter readings.

General formula. A formula which accounts for any member of a particular *homologous series**. For example, the general formula of all *alkenes** is C_nH_{2n}. Ethene has two carbon atoms and twice as many hydrogen atoms as it does carbon atoms. Therefore it has a *chemical formula** of C_2H_4. Propene has three carbon atoms, and so its chemical formula is C_3H_6.

*Solvent, 50; Isotopes, 7; Relative atomic mass, 7; Mole, 28; Radioactivity, 48; Ionize, 12; Homologous series, 42; Alkenes, 43; Chemical formula, 3.

Heavy metals. Metals with a high density, such as lead, mercury and tungsten.

Hydroxide. A substance containing the ion, OH^-. The OH^- ion is negative and causes alkalinity. All alkalis contain OH^- ions. Most hydroxides, with the exceptions of ammonium, potassium, sodium and lithium, are insoluble.

Ignite. To start the process of *combustion**, usually with a spark. The **ignition temperature** of a substance is the lowest temperature at which that substance will combust.

Kelvin. A standard unit of temperature change, named after the scientist, Lord Kelvin. It has the symbol K. One unit Kelvin equals one degree Celsius.

Liquefaction. A change in state, from gas to liquid, of a substance that is a gas at room temperature. This is achieved by cooling and increasing pressure.

Mass. The amount of matter in a substance. Mass is measured in grams and kilograms.

Mineral. A material that occurs naturally but does not come from animals or plants. For example, metal ores, limestone and coal are all minerals.

Oxide. A compound formed by the combination of an element and oxygen only, such as calcium oxide (CaO).

Phosphates. *Salts** of phosphoric acid (H_3PO_4). They are used in fertilizers to replace the phosphorus used up by intensive farming.

Precipitate. An insoluble solid which separates from a solution during a chemical reaction. In the reaction below, lead(II) chloride is left as a precipitate.

$$Pb(NO_3)_2 + 2NaCl \rightarrow PbCl_2 + NaNO_3$$
Lead(II)   Sodium   Lead(II)   Sodium
nitrate   chloride   chloride   nitrate

Promoter. Also called an **activator**, this increases the efficiency of a *catalyst**. For example, in the Haber process, the transition metal, molybdenum (Mo), increases the activity of the catalyst iron.

Proteins. A naturally-occurring *polymer** made from chains of *monomers** called **amino acids**. Proteins are used by living cells for growth and the repair of living tissue.

PTFE. An abbreviation for poly(tetrafluoroethene), PTFE is a polymer used as a non-stick, low friction coating on saucepans, frisbees and vehicle bearings.

Raw materials. A substance used at the start of a large-scale chemical process which is converted into a product required by industry. For example, sand, lead(II) oxide and calcium oxide are the raw materials needed to make lead glass.

Sediment. The solid which settles in a *suspension** The speed at which the sediment collects can be used to determine the average size of the suspension particles.

Solvay process. A process which takes limestone ($CaCO_3(s)$) and brine ($2NaCl(aq)$) and converts them into sodium carbonate ($Na_2CO_3(aq)$) and calcium chloride $CaCl_2(aq)$). The process involves many stages but is a cheap way of producing the valuable alkali, sodium carbonate, from readily available resources.

Sublimation. The change of state from a solid to a gas without passing through the liquid state. For example, graphite sublimes at a temperature of 3730 °C.

Surface tension The tendency of the surface of a liquid to act as if it was covered by a skin. This is due to the force of attraction between the surface molecules.

Synthesis. The formation of a substance from simpler substances. The term **synthetic** usually applies to an artificial or man made substance.

Tarnish. To lose shine due to the formation of a dull surface layer. Many metals tarnish when left in contact with the air for a long period of time.

Volume. A measurement of the amount of space occupied by a substance. Volume is usually measured in cubic centimetres (cm^3).

Vulcanization. The process of heating raw natural rubber with sulphur. Vulcanized rubber is harder, tougher and less temperature sensitive than ordinary rubber.

Waves. When an object disturbs its immediate environment, the disturbance travels away from the source in the form of waves. Gamma ray radiation is a form of wave. Other types of wave include light and radio waves.

*Combustion, 10; Salts, 26; Catalyst, 35; Polymer, 44; Monomer, 44, Suspension, 50.

Laboratory apparatus

Equipment used in the laboratory is called **apparatus**. In exams and text books apparatus is usually drawn in a specific, two dimensional way. Below are some common pieces of apparatus.

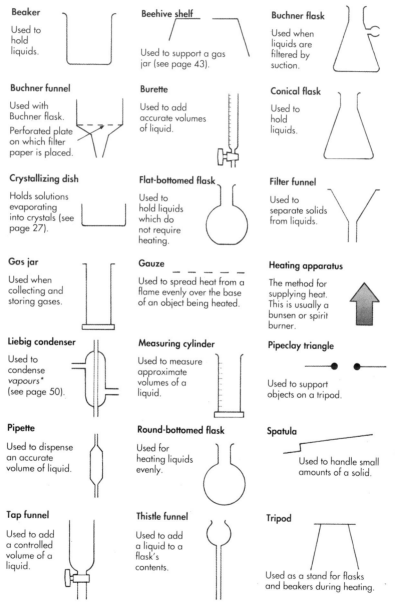

Beaker

Used to hold liquids.

Beehive shelf

Used to support a gas jar (see page 43).

Buchner flask

Used when liquids are filtered by suction.

Buchner funnel

Used with Buchner flask.

Perforated plate on which filter paper is placed.

Burette

Used to add accurate volumes of liquid.

Conical flask

Used to hold liquids.

Crystallizing dish

Holds solutions evaporating into crystals (see page 27).

Flat-bottomed flask

Used to hold liquids which do not require heating.

Filter funnel

Used to separate solids from liquids.

Gas jar

Used when collecting and storing gases.

Gauze

Used to spread heat from a flame evenly over the base of an object being heated.

Heating apparatus

The method for supplying heat. This is usually a bunsen or spirit burner.

Liebig condenser

Used to condense *vapours** (see page 50).

Measuring cylinder

Used to measure approximate volumes of a liquid.

Pipeclay triangle

Used to support objects on a tripod.

Pipette

Used to dispense an accurate volume of liquid.

Round-bottomed flask

Used for heating liquids evenly.

Spatula

Used to handle small amounts of a solid.

Tap funnel

Used to add a controlled volume of a liquid.

Thistle funnel

Used to add a liquid to a flask's contents.

Tripod

Used as a stand for flasks and beakers during heating.

Index

First published in 1992 by Usborne Publishing Ltd, 83-85 Saffron Hill, London EC1N 8RT, England.

The name Usborne and the device ☂ are trade marks of Usborne Publishing Ltd. Printed in Spain.

UE